I0736768

HOW TO CATCH A BIKER

SPECIAL EDITION

CHESTER FALLS
BOOK FIVE

ANA ASHLEY

Illustrated by
COVERS BY JULES

Cover design: Covers by Jules

Editor: Abbie Nicole

Join Ana's Facebook Group *facebook.com/groups/CafeRoMMance* for exclusive content, and to learn more about her latest books at *anawritesmm.com*!

DEDICATION

Dear Froglet,

We've got this!

Poppet

ABOUT HOW TO CATCH A BIKER

What do you do when you meet the tall, gruff silver fox of your dreams?
You flirt, pretend it didn't happen, and secretly admire his assets.
For research purposes, of course.
I came to Chester Falls to find my voice and save my publishing career.
Instead, I find him.
Slade's story is kept under a lock so strong I don't know if there is a man out there that can break it.
But I'll be damned if I won't give it a try.

A biker with a past
A down-in-the-dumps author
A kitten with a tiger attitude
Two guys that discover there isn't that much mileage between reality and fiction.
How to Catch a Biker is the fifth book in the Chester Falls series and features a May/December story between two guys who have more in common than they think, a group of friends who think everyone needs to be in love, and a small town like no other.

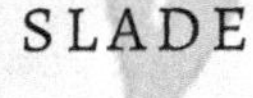

SLADE

"*H*ey, baby."

What the fuck.

I glanced at the screen on my phone to double-check that I hadn't been stupid enough to answer a call from my ex.

Unknown Number.

"Slade, honey? Are you there?" he asked in that sweet, deep voice he thought still worked for me. It had, once upon a time, many times over.

"What do you want, Mike?" I tried to keep my voice flat. I knew he'd pick on up the slightest hint of emotion and latch onto it.

"Now, now, baby. That's no way to greet your husband—"

"Ex-husband, Mike. Ex. Husband," I said, failing to take the bite out of my voice.

"That's why I'm calling," he said.

"What do you mean? And make it quick, I have work to get to."

"It's our anniversary."

"I'm hanging up."

"Wait," he said. "Please..." His voice changed, and I knew I was going to regret it, but I waited until the silence became too heavy, even for me.

"Mike..."

"I just...do you remember that day? Can you believe it was twenty-five years ago? It was so hot and sticky. The hottest day in Atlanta that summer. I was running late for work, but when I saw you, leaning against your bike wearing that leather jacket as if you were too cool to feel the heat..." he chuckled.

How could I not remember? It was the day my life changed forever, and not just for the reason he liked to remember.

"It was a good day," I confessed.

Mike's memory of the guy across the road from where he worked in his uncle's garage couldn't be further from reality.

I'd been scared and unsure. I'd wanted to cross the road and trust that the promises I'd been given weren't as empty as the tank on my trusted Harley.

Instead, I was given a job, and I'd met the man that taught me my life could be good, or at least better than it had been until then. That is until he broke my heart and my trust.

"You were always a mystery, Slade. It was exciting at first, but then..."

I sighed. "Why are we having this conversation? You were the one who left, and not before you took everything you wanted and more."

"Slade..."

"Look, I don't know what you want from this trip down memory lane, but I've moved on. I live on Reality Avenue, where I have a business to run. I suggest you go back to whatever twink you're fucking this week and leave me alone."

I ended the call before he could say anything else.

These days, the only person I kept my mouth shut for was my bank manager, so it was definitely a good idea to end the call.

It was the hottest day of the summer so far, making the

glass walls of my office feel like a fishbowl under a UV light, but Mike's interruption only delayed the work I needed to do today, so I grabbed a bottle of water from my small office fridge and drank it all in one go.

The satisfaction of closing my spreadsheets one hour later was only matched by the information they contained within. My business was doing well. So well, in fact, that maybe I could offer Liam a few more hours and consider finally taking the time to work on my bike restoration.

I stepped outside the office. Liam was in the garage working under a car and whistling a tune I didn't recognize.

The familiar smell of oil, grease, paint, and sweat calmed me down, and since there were no customers in the shop, I allowed myself the moment to enjoy the feeling of rightness whenever I was in my workspace. The garage, *not* the office. That was merely a necessary part of running a business.

When I'd seen this building only around the corner from the Chester Falls main square, I knew I'd found my perfect place.

The vintage bike shop with the adjacent garage had direct access from the main street, attracting curious passersby as well as my loyal customers.

Cars weren't really my thing, so when Liam had walked in asking for a job, just a couple of months after I'd opened the shop, I hadn't cared that I had no clue how to pay him.

As it turned out, he'd worked for the previous owners, and since there was no other garage in town, we had a captive audience. As much as I'd wanted to run an exclusive vintage bike repair and restoration shop, I knew it was smart to diversify.

I'd been dumb too many times in my life to not know when to smarten up.

The shop was exactly how I'd always wanted. Paved flooring, a few display cabinets, a leather couch, and several blown-up photos of vintage bikes on the walls.

It was big enough to have a good range of bikes on display,

mostly Harleys, but it still felt cozy and personable. Most of all, the long glass wall behind the bikes gave my customers a direct view of the garage.

"Hey, boss," Liam said, sliding out from under the car. "I put the new alternator in Mrs. Mason's car. I'll just give it a quick once over and it'll be good to go."

"That's great. Thanks, Liam. You can head home when you finish."

"You sure? I can hang around," he said, wiping his greasy hands on a rag.

"I'm sure."

"You know Maggie will bring you coffee whether or not you let me off early."

Liam was a good ten years younger than me, and after losing his first wife at a young age, he'd found love again in the girl that seemed to come by a little too often for someone who didn't own a car, bike, or even had a driver's license.

Maggie was a sweet girl in her mid-twenties, and as long as she kept bringing us coffee from Spilled Beans, she could pop by to visit Liam any time. Or have him home early as the case may be.

"I have no ulterior motive. Just being nice," I said, raising my hands.

I wasn't kidding anyone. Indy's coffee was the best and, on most days, we were so busy that Maggie's treat was a lifesaver.

"All right, then. Will we see you at the book fair later?" he asked.

I'd almost forgotten about the fair. These days, reading was my only form of relaxation, usually before I fell asleep after a long day at the shop.

"Maybe," I said. "I want to catch up on some things, but I'll drop by."

I went over to the main shop while Liam finished up. Working with cars and bikes was a messy and smelly business.

Just because the scent of oil got my engine running, it didn't mean the general public agreed with it, so I'd made sure that my staff facilities had a locker room with a shower and the best oil removing soap available.

Liam was my only employee, but the way things were going, I could see myself hiring a couple more people in the next year or so. Especially if it meant I wouldn't need to get anywhere near a car.

I glanced at the corner of the garage where my passion project stood covered up and waiting for me to get my head out of my ass and start working on it.

"All right, boss. I'll see you later," Liam said, coming into the shop area looking fresh as a daisy.

I waved him off.

"Hey, Liam," I said, just as he reached the front door. "I don't suppose you'd want to pick up a few more hours?"

He grinned widely. "You serious, boss?"

I nodded.

"Hell yeah, I'll do it. I'm saving to get Maggie a nice ring. I know we haven't been going out long, but when you know, you know. Right?"

"You can't let a girl like Maggie get away, that's for sure."

He nodded and left with the biggest smile on his face.

My mind went back to the call from Mike. I once thought we had forever too.

Saying life after my parents died wasn't easy was the understatement of the century, so when I met him, he was the ray of sunshine I craved. If he was a flower, I was a bee drunk on his sweet nectar.

Except I carried secrets I had never been able to share and, in the end, that broke us. Yes, he'd cheated, but when you hide who you really are from the person you love, aren't you as much of a cheater?

We normally didn't get many customers in the shop on

Saturday mornings, so I busied myself putting things away in the garage and closing it before heading back to close the shop.

I stole another glance at the old Harley and then pulled out the list of parts I needed to order for it. I reckoned I could have it ready by the end of the summer, when I usually closed the shop for a week to get out on the open road.

The thought alone caused my skin to erupt in excited goosebumps. I'd missed out on the trip last year, when I'd come down with an unexpected flu, so I wanted to make this year count.

I pulled out my phone and blocked the number Mike had called me from. I wasn't interested in living in the past.

The man that had saved my life said to me once, "*Slade, son, nothing good comes from looking back. Put the good memories in a safe box and move forward. Only when you're miles away from the past, can you afford to look back inside the box and pick a memory to revisit. Don't do it too early, or you'll be tempted to turn around. Make sure you're far away enough that you can't.*"

Those words had carried me from Seattle to Atlanta and then to Chester Falls.

When I'd arrived in the small town six years ago, I thought I'd stepped into a place that wasn't made for people like me. It was too nice, too perfect.

Time showed me that people here were as flawed as anywhere else, and so, a day at a time, I carved out my little spot in the community.

After locking everything up, I went around the building to the outside stairs that lead up to my apartment above the store. I liked that there was a separation. My apartment was my sanctuary. There, I didn't have any secrets. I could open my memory box and bring back the good ones any time I liked.

One scan of my bookshelf reminded me that I'd recently donated some books to Goodwill, so what a perfect day to fill it up with new ones.

Maybe I'd bump into Liam and Maggie at the book fair.
Maybe I'd buy her an iced coffee.

Now those were memories I wanted to make.

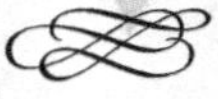

"*A*iden, I didn't know you were in town." Ben's smile was as warm as always, but the strain on his arms from carrying a big, heavy box of books was written all over his face.

"Wait, let me help you," I said, taking the box from him. "Where do you want it?"

"Outside, in the square," he said. "You see that gazebo in the middle? That's where we're taking the books."

Bookmarked, Ben's bookstore, was always busy on a Saturday morning, and since the front door had been open when I came in, I didn't even notice the sign was flipped to closed. There was also an unusual number of boxes filled with books by the checkout desk.

"What's going on out there?" I asked.

"It's the Summer Book Fair. We do it every year, but this year is a special one," Ben said, walking past me with another box of books and indicating for me to follow.

"Why is that?"

"It's our twentieth anniversary. My Aunt Jackie started it to offload older books and raise money for town projects."

We crossed the road into the square that always seemed to be the center of the town of Chester Falls.

"That's such an amazing idea," I said.

"Yeah." He put his box down by a few others, and I followed his example. "I still remember the first one she ever organized. It was just a table outside the store with a small sign. The money she raised was enough to pay for catering and some costumes for the school's nativity play. The next year she had more books, and the year after that people asked if they could donate books to raise more money."

"So it's like a big philanthropic book exchange," I said.

Ben grinned. "Precisely."

As we approached the middle of the square, I saw piles of boxes filled with books ready to be displayed on the rows of tables that were already set up under the shade of the gazebo.

It was a warm summer day without a hint of a breeze. Beads of sweat ran down my forehead and I felt them on the small of my back too, but I felt better and more useful than I had in a long time.

"Oh gosh, I didn't mean to put you to work before you even had a chance to say good morning," Ben said, wiping his face with the back of his hand. "Especially not in this heat. We're always lucky with the weather, but this year is definitely warmer. It's a good thing Indy is setting up a stand with cool drinks."

"It's my pleasure to help. You said books and charity in one sentence. If that's not right up my alley, I don't know what is," I said as we walked back to Bookmarked. "Sounds like I picked the right time to visit. Can I help out in any way? Other than helping you carry the rest of the boxes, of course."

We were back inside the store. Ben gave me an assessing gaze that I tried to ignore by bending down to pick up another box.

"Aiden, don't get me wrong, because it's always great to see you, but does anyone know you're here?"

I put the box down and sat on it.

My best friend, Wren, had moved back home to Chester Falls from San Diego eighteen months ago. Since then, I'd visited the small town a number of times and had come to know his extended group of friends, including Ben and his husband, Tristan.

They were the reason I'd come straight to Bookmarked, rather than the store next door, Fabulize, which happened to belong to Wren's fiancé, Tom.

"I...um..." I let out a tired breath, unsure of how much to say.

"For an author, you are strangely out of words," Ben said. He crouched down next to me. While his tone carried a hint of amusement, I could tell he was genuinely concerned, or maybe just curious.

Everyone was used to seeing Aiden, the successful author who had his shit together.

Nothing could be further from the truth.

"I was wondering if Tristan knows anyone who might have an apartment to rent short-term."

Tristan was an interior designer and had moved here from Boston a couple of years ago. I'd heard enough stories from their group of friends to know Tristan worked with a lot of landlords in the local area.

Ben's eyes bugged out. "You want to move here? But how about Rich—"

I shook my head. That was something I really did not want to talk about right now. Outside, the perfect day awaited us, and I was so fucking tired from my own life, I really needed to work on something positive and fun for a change.

"I'm just working on a new book, that's all, and I could do with a change of scenery while I do it."

Ben nodded and stood up, grabbing his phone from the desk.

"Tristan is with a client, but I sent him a message. Do you have anywhere to stay tonight?" he asked.

"I checked a local hotel, and they have plenty of vacancies if I can't get a place."

"You know you can stay with us, right? The couch is quite comfortable. Let's not even mention that Wren and Tom might be upset if they know you're in a hotel and not staying with them."

Yes, I knew that, which was why I wanted to find a place to stay first. Because as much as I loved the generosity of my friends, the last thing I wanted was to be in close proximity to a loved-up couple.

So much for being a romance author. These days I struggled with even the concept of love.

"I'll cross that bridge when the time comes." I stood up. "Should we get back to work?"

Ben squeezed my shoulder and picked up the box next to me.

"That's it," Ben said a few trips later as we stood under the blissful shade of the gazebo. "Each box has a genre label that matches the signs on the table. All you need to do is stack the books neatly so people can read the titles on the spine."

"Got it, boss."

Over the next hour we worked on the book displays. I made sure to stay away from the romance section because it was a surefire way of getting distracted. I'd have time to scan through the titles later.

A small crowd gathered around the square, eager to check out the books on offer.

Indy opened up his cold-drinks stand, which included his new special-blend iced coffee. I'd been to his coffee shop, Spilled Beans, enough times to know I needed to get my hands on one of those coffees.

As soon as we cleared the space from all the empty boxes, Ben declared the fair open, giving a little speech about his aunt and how happy she'd be to see her project still alive after all these years.

My little writer heart jumped for joy seeing everyone happily scanning through the books and buying more than a few.

"Hey, guys, sorry, I'm late. Charlotte wanted to come with me, so Hannah and I had to use some diverting tactics," Ellie, Ben's business partner, said joining us. "Give me another six months, and I'll be ready to graduate from ninja school with honors."

We laughed. I'd met eighteen-month-old Charlotte before, and she was a bundle of energy and unparalleled cuteness.

"Nice to see you, Aiden. I didn't know you were coming to the fair," she said.

I rubbed the back of my neck, a little embarrassed at the reminder that I'd turned up unannounced.

Fortunately, Ben jumped in the conversation. "It was a last-minute thing. I messaged him about the fair, and the next thing I knew...poof, he's here."

"Oh...my...bubblegum-flavored ice cream with a cherry on top."

I put a smile I didn't feel on my face and turned around to face Tom, whose eyes were on my designer shirt. He came closer and started stroking the fabric on the sleeve.

"Holy mother of pearls, this feels beautiful," he said and kissed my cheek. "Nice to see you, Aiden."

"Hi, Tom."

Tom's literal sparkling personality brought a smile to my lips, but it soon died down when I saw Wren's frown.

"Baby, why don't you grab us an iced coffee from Indy?" he said to Tom.

"Coffee for everyone with cream and sprinkles coming right up," Tom said before walking away.

Ben and Ellie both made themselves scarce.

Great. Thanks, guys.

"What's going on?" Wren asked.

"Nothing's going on, what do you mean?"

"You're in Chester Falls."

I looked around and smiled. "Yup."

"Why didn't you say you were coming?" he asked, not bothering to hide the hurt in his voice.

"Surprise!"

"You're staying with us," he declared, crossing his arms in front of his chest.

"Wren—"

"No, something's going on, and if you don't want to talk about it, that's okay. But you're my best friend and I want to be here for you."

Even though I already knew that, his words still meant more than he could possibly imagine.

"Thank you, but I have a place to stay already," I lied.

"How long are you staying?"

"Maybe a few weeks? I'm researching for a new book."

"Weeks?" His frown gave turn to a wide grin that made his light-blue eyes shine even brighter. "Man, this is going to be great. I've gotten my running buddy back."

I laughed.

"Don't laugh. By the time I'm done with you, you'll be moving here permanently."

As much as the idea had some appeal, I wasn't sure I was ready to move away from San Diego. That felt too permanent. Final.

SLADE

There wasn't much a cold shower on a hot day couldn't fix, in my opinion, so thirty minutes after closing the shop for the weekend, I was feeling refreshed and ready to head out.

I hadn't missed a single book fair since I'd moved to Chester Falls, and as soon as I turned the corner from my street onto the square, I could tell this year's fair was bigger and better.

There was a line for Indy's iced coffee stand, and a separate one spilling from his coffee shop onto the street. The main event of the day was the book fair, but no one in Chester Falls would go without a cold drink and a pastry.

Not that I could blame them, Indy's cakes were the best, even though I didn't indulge in them often. Being in the shop all day didn't leave me much time to work out and, at forty-eight, my body didn't bounce back from a sugar-filled diet in the same way it had when I was younger.

Maybe I'd grab a pastry to take home for later, but I didn't want my hands busy with drinks and food while I scanned through the books.

That was my mission for the afternoon, to fill up my bookshelf with as many romance novels as I could carry home.

As they say, those who can't, teach. With me, it's more a case of those who can't romance, read about it.

I moved through the small crowd, smiling and nodding my greetings to the locals I already knew well. It never ceased to amaze me how welcoming everyone was. If I didn't know better, I would think I'd lived here all my life.

Wren Mason, the high school coach, waved from where he stood with Tom near Indy's stand. His eyes lit up, but I smiled and shook my head at him. He grinned and came over.

"Oh, come on, Slade," he said.

"I'm too old, Wren. The only group sport I'm interested in is the kind I watch on PornHub."

He snorted. Since Wren had moved back to Chester Falls, he'd been on a mission to get the whole town involved in some kind of sport or physical activity. The kids' football team was currently winning their league, and as a former professional player, that was probably not enough winning for him.

He was starting an adult football team, and maybe he hadn't had enough young people join because now he was coming after the old farts, like me, too.

"It's only for fun, Slade. Let out some steam after a day of hard work at the shop. It'll be great."

"My fun after a hard day's work includes a beer and one of the books I'll be buying today." I patted his shoulder and carried on toward the gazebo. He seemed a little deflated by my refusal, and I almost felt bad for not joining him in his excitement, but football had never really been my thing.

As I'd predicted, this year's book assortment was bigger than last year's, and the romance section had doubled in size.

Trying to get to it was a challenge in itself, but at least on this occasion, my six-foot-four height was an advantage. I moved through the tables, peering over people's shoulders to see if I recognized any of my favorite authors.

A glance over the thriller section proved fruitless, but it was useful in biding my time until the crowd moved away from my favorite genre.

I waved at Ben, who was at the other end of the gazebo busy ringing through all the purchases. We were both on the Chester Falls Chamber of Commerce and often discussed our favorite romance novels between meeting breaks.

He'd been a little shy at first. A reaction I often got from people that didn't know me, but once he'd gotten past the height, the beard, and the rough exterior, he didn't stop talking about books until I confessed my love for gay romance. We even shared the same favorite author.

I moved out of the way of a little girl holding a bunch of children's books and an ice cream, just in time to avoid wearing it on my jeans.

As the girl ran to her mother with the ice cream miraculously still attached to the wafer cone, I let out a relieved breath and turned back to the table.

A book I'd been wanting to read for a while caught my eye. It had mixed reviews, but the blurb had caught my attention when I read it online.

I reached out for it just in time to get caught in a tug-of-war with someone else over the book.

"I'm sor—" My gaze followed the soft, pale skin of the hand gripping my book. The guy's shirtsleeves were rolled up, which showed off his slim but defined forearms, though not nearly enough.

I kept looking up until I met with chestnut-brown eyes that even behind the slim dark-metal frames were deep and assessing.

"I'm sorry. You have it, you went for it first," he said, pushing the book in my direction.

"No, no, you have it."

"No, honestly, it's okay."

I took the book, since he didn't seem prepared to relent.

"I'm not even sure I'll like it," I said. "I've read the reviews online."

He smiled. "That's exactly why I wanted to read it too."

"Please, I insist." I gave him the book and, that time, he took it.

His face seemed familiar, but I couldn't place it. We definitely hadn't met before because I knew I'd have remembered. With his sharp jaw and soft eyes, he looked like he could take me out with one look and then hug me to make up for it.

The back of my neck felt hot. Hell, it wasn't just the back of my neck, and I don't think I could blame it entirely on the weather.

Putting it simply, the guy was stunning, even if he was far too young for me. And those eyes... God, they could probably pry the deepest secrets out of me without even trying.

I definitely needed to move my attention back to my book-finding mission.

"Well, enjoy the book," I said, picking up a random novel without checking the title or author name.

"Maybe..." he trailed.

I looked up at him. He tilted his head and bit his lip, and my dick enjoyed the image far too much.

A tiny blush appeared under the collar of his shirt, and I wondered if his skin was as soft and pale all over. He was probably some kind of lawyer or accountant. Someone who spent his life indoors.

Suddenly I felt the urge to invite him for a ride on my bike, just so I could see what he'd look like with his skin flushed from the adrenaline of being on the road.

"I'm staying in town for a little while, maybe you can borrow the book when I'm finished with it?" The question took me by surprise.

"I'm sure Ben has more copies of the book," I said, immediately regretting it when the guy flinched.

"Oh...yeah, of course. Well, um...happy book hunting." He turned around to face another row of books.

"I'm sorry, that came out all wrong," I said.

"It's okay, I know when I'm being dismissed. Just for the record, I wasn't flirting."

He walked away, and I knew I should have gone back to the books, but my legs decided for me by chasing after him.

"Hey," I said, grabbing his wrist. It was such a bad idea because just the feel of his soft skin under my rough hands made all the heat from the earth's core climb up my arm. "For the record, I wasn't dismissing you."

"Right." He pulled his hand back and put it in the pocket of his jeans.

I tried not to stare, but for all the self-restraint I had, I never claimed to be a saint.

"People aren't really my thing," I said.

He looked around us and raised his brows.

I laughed. "I'm fine with crowds. It's single people I'm not as good with."

"What makes you think I'm single?"

I opened my mouth and shut it again.

He laughed. "Relax, I was only joking. Let's start from the beginning."

I nodded, still not trusting anything else out of my mouth while in the presence of this guy that somehow got my gut all twisted.

"Hi, I'm Aiden, and I love books. I think you do too. I'm kinda new in town, so if you're free any time, we could meet up for a coffee and talk about this book we both want to read. Oh, and I'm single but not looking for a relationship. Just putting it out there."

It took me a moment to notice his outstretched hand between us. I met it with mine, ignoring again how nice it felt. I definitely needed another shower when I got home.

"Nice to meet you, Aiden. Maybe I'll see you around."

"Maybe..."

He smiled and left me staring at his ass as he walked away toward the checkout desk Ben had set up for the fair.

It was hard to focus on any books after that, so I picked a few random titles and paid for them before heading back home. I didn't bother seeing Liam and Maggie or buying a pastry from Spilled Beans.

The second shower did a good job of cooling me down before I put my new books away on the shelf. One of my favorites, one I could never give away to Goodwill, caught my attention, so I pulled it out from the shelf and sat on my couch.

The sunlight from the tall window in my living room made my couch the perfect reading nook, so I made myself comfortable and opened the book to the first page.

Some days it was better revisiting old friends than meeting new ones, even when they had deep, brown eyes that sucked you in and promised to keep you warm.

My hands stilled and my heartbeat increased when my eyes stopped on the author photo on the inside of the cover.

Brown eyes, this time without the glasses but unmistakably deep and soft, stared back at me. Aiden was A. Lawton. All that time when I thought I recognized Aiden but couldn't place him.

"I'm such an idiot." I groaned.

Now I definitely couldn't read the book. That's how deep my embarrassment level was.

I just hoped he wasn't staying in town for too long. Maybe if I kept to myself and didn't leave the shop, I'd avoid bumping into him. That seemed like a good idea, and I had my bike restoration to work on, anyway. I'd be plenty busy with that.

I was definitely not going to think about how I'd embarrassed myself in front of the man who was responsible for so many of my lost hours, heartbreaks, and happy-ever-afters.

AIDEN

I should have known I'd be ambushed. I should have recognized the first sign a mile away.

After all, how many times had I written a main character being coerced into facing their issues by well-intentioned friends?

The answer was too many to count, but enough that I should have known when it was happening to me.

"What did you think of the fair?" Wren asked.

I raised a brow. Was that really what he wanted to ask me? Okay, then.

"It was great. I was only recognized a couple of times, and now I have a handful of books to read."

I raised the menu high enough to cover my face and started reading through the options. Indy had been generous enough to offer me one of his amazing pastries earlier, but that had been too many conversations and forced smiles ago.

"I'm torn between having breakfast for dinner or a burger that'll send me to my grave too early. I could do both. I always wondered what my mother would wear to my funeral," I said.

After wrapping up the fair, Wren had cornered me inside Bookmarked and more or less given me no choice but to follow him to Benny's Diner. His excuse? We needed to save a table for everyone because it was Saturday and the diner always got busy.

I looked around. He was half right, which also meant he was half wrong. Most people picked one of the booths by the window, so the bigger tables in the middle of the diner were empty, apart from the one we'd claimed.

"Have one today and the other tomorrow. After all, you're staying in town," he said.

I bit my lip to stop from laughing. He was trying so hard to raise the subject without raising it.

"Yeah, I could do that."

"So what are you working on? You said it's a new book."

"Yup."

He let out a frustrated sigh. "You're really not going to tell me what's going on?"

Wren's big heart was what drew me to him when we kept bumping into each other on our daily runs on the beach in San Diego. Even before we'd officially met, he'd already done enough little things that showed me how good he was.

His car was bigger than mine, so when he would get to the beach parking lot before me, he'd pick one spot away from the corner, which made the free space harder to see unless you knew it was already there. If he saw me running without any water, he'd leave a new bottle by the front wheel of my car.

Somehow I'd never felt sexual attraction toward him, and not just because all the time we'd known each other I'd been in a relationship. Wren was gorgeous, but to me he was like the big brother I'd never had. So I'd declared him my friend and introduced myself to him.

"Fine." I gave in. "I don't want to worry you, and I know Tom will cut off my balls if he thinks you're upset because of me."

"You're not wrong there. You really don't want me to be upset." He pursed his lips, which was a ridiculous expression for someone his size, although I'm sure that worked on Tom all the time.

"Richard and I broke up—"

"Thank fuck."

I stared at him.

"Sorry, was that too soon? Oh my god, are you hurting? I mean, he was a douchey dickwaffle, but I know you had feelings for him." He ran his hand through his short hair. "Fuck. I'm sorry, Aid, I am...shit."

"That was a little too quick, I'll admit, but you're not wrong. He is all those things, it just took me a long time to realize it."

"What happened?"

"He proposed."

Wren opened his mouth but was interrupted by the larger-than-life owner and namesake of the diner, Benny.

"Well, look who we have here. If I'd known we were having a celebrity in the house, I would have made a cake."

I laughed. "Word on the street is that you're not allowed in the kitchen."

"Yeah, yeah, the fire department has no sense of humor. Anyway, what can I get you? I'm assuming you're waiting for the gang, so let's start with drinks."

We went for a beer each and Wren asked for a bowl of nachos to snack on until everyone else arrived. I wasn't sure who everyone else was, but I suspected that Ben and Tristan would come and so would Indy and his husband, Tate. And Tom, of course. That he wasn't here already, grilling me, told me exactly how worried Wren really was.

Wren turned to me as soon as Benny left. "What do you mean, he proposed? And don't get me wrong; I think it's good you're not with him, but how do you go from a proposal to a breakup?"

"Easy, he didn't propose to me."

If I had a camera on hand I'd have taken a photo of Wren's

face, but my phone was in my pocket, and as soon as I laughed, he changed his confused expression to a scowl.

"He proposed to my mother, assuming I'd say yes. Her monthly calls became weekly and then daily. She was cagey whenever I asked her about it. At some point I wondered if she had a terminal illness. Then one day she let it slip that she'd booked the Plaza in New York."

"Are you joking?"

"I wish I was. I asked Richard about it, and that's when he confessed his plan to take me to New York on our anniversary and get married the same day."

Benny brought our drinks, and I drank half of my beer in one go.

"Hey, don't do anything silly, okay? We don't have to talk about this," Wren said.

"Don't worry, I won't drink myself stupid. After all, I still have no clue where I'm staying tonight. Tristan said he had the keys to an apartment I could use. Apparently the owner is traveling, and her parents are quite happy that someone will keep an eye on it."

The guys all turned up at the same time, which put an end to our conversation. The look Wren threw my way told me it wasn't over.

Somehow just saying what happened aloud made me feel a little better, a little less alone. Even though we hadn't gotten to the best part of the story yet. It was just a shame that, unlike the books I wrote, this one didn't have a happy-ever-after.

The noise level at the diner went up a few decibels with the guys all talking over each other to put their orders in. How Benny kept track of any of it was beyond me. I'd asked for the double cheeseburger with bacon and Momma Ruth's special sauce, but I was hungry enough that I'd eat anything he put in front of me.

With the orders in and the center of the table filled with

drinks for everyone, five pairs of eyes stared at me. Wren gave me a break by focusing on Tom instead.

"Don't look at me like that. I basically saved your asses by turning up today. Don't question it," I said.

They all laughed and lifted their drinks for a toast.

"I'm beat, but it was so worth it," Ben said, leaning against Tristan, who put an arm over his shoulder and kissed his head.

"Uh huh," Indy muttered. Tate had his fingers laced through the back of Indy's hair and was massaging the scalp under the dark-blue hair he always wore tied up in a bun.

I studied everyone and wondered how soon I could leave without seeming rude. After all, they were all nice enough, but there was just too much love around the table, and not all of it was contained within couples.

Not to mention that after a week of traveling and staying in random hotels, I was dying for a real bed with bedsheets that hadn't been slept in by thousands of people.

"What I want to know is what kind of book you're writing?"

The question came from Tom, and was so out of the blue, I had to look around to make sure I'd heard correctly.

"Oh, don't be so surprised. I read," he said with indignation.

"Fashion magazines don't count, babe," Wren said.

Tom gave him a pointed stare and then turned to me again. "Okay, I'm being nosy, but I'm also asking what everyone wants to know but doesn't have the sparkles to ask."

He definitely had the sparkles all right. Tom was such an infectiously positive human, I was pretty sure there wasn't a single person who would deny him anything.

"I only have half a plot bunny, but this character won't leave me alone. Thing is, he's a biker, and I have no clue about biker culture or bikes. I've done as much research on the internet as I can, but something tells me I need to find someone who lives that life. I just don't know where to start."

They all looked at each other.

"I know someone you can talk to here in town," Wren said.

"Really? That would be great."

"Slade owns the vintage bike store in town. I'm picking up mom's car from him on Monday, so I can take you there."

I nodded and munched on a couple of nachos.

Slade...good name.

Would he have a beard? Leather jacket? Cloudy blue eyes that hid a secret?

My thoughts ran away from me, until I realized in my head I was describing the sexy, older man I'd met earlier. He'd left without giving me a name.

Maybe it was for the best. He could be the mysterious inspiration for my new character...Slade.

SLADE

"Fuck!"

"Slade?"

"Out here," I answered from under the fucking car.

Liam had gone out to Spilled Beans to get us coffee, and in my misplaced sense of teamwork, I decided to change the oil filter in a car we'd had in this morning with an oil leak. Liam was probably going to kill me and ask me to stop helping out and stick to working on the bikes.

I hated working with cars. They were messy, bulky, and had a lot less class than a Harley, in my opinion. No one ever looked sexy driving a car...unless it was an Aston Martin, of course.

Sadly, that was not the kind of car I was unlucky enough to get stuck under while doing the simplest task in the world and still managing to spill oil all over my shirt.

"Oh man, so many jokes, such a small audience," Wren said. I didn't need to see him to recognize his voice.

"Hey, respect your elders. You're here for your mom's car?"

"I was, but now I'm wondering what filming a mechanic coming out from under a car all rugged and oil stained will do to my sex life."

I replaced the drain plug and tightened it. That was the end of the messy job, now I just needed to fit the new filter.

"Put that phone away or I'll charge you double. Besides, with the smooshy-happy face Tom goes around with, I didn't think you had any problems with your sex life."

I heard two sets of chuckles. Considering the way he was joking, I assumed Wren was with someone we both knew. Or at least I hoped he was.

The last thing I needed was for a new customer to hear the exchange and have a bad impression of me and my business.

Not that they'd get a better one once they saw me wearing engine oil on a T-shirt that would never be white again.

I slid out from under the car. "Thanks for waiting, Wren. Let me just change this shirt before I—" The rest of my words became lodged in my throat, as thick as the oil coating my clothes. Because right there next to Wren, was the owner of those brown eyes that had haunted my dirty dreams all weekend.

A. Lawton...Aiden.

He grinned. "We meet again. Did you have a chance to read the book?"

I looked at him and then Wren, who was staring back at me with strange interest.

"You two know each other?" Wren asked.

"Yes, we met on Saturday at the fair, but I was short-changed," he said.

"How so?" I asked, trying to ignore the fact that A. fucking Lawton stood in front of me like an advertisement for fashionable casual clothing while I was a mess.

"I never got your name."

His gaze scanned over me. If this was another place, and he was another man, I'd think he was undressing me with his eyes, but he looked like he was cataloguing me as if he wanted to remember all the details down to the shape of the oil stains on my shirt.

I followed his gaze. He wasn't wearing his glasses today, which I thought was a shame.

He stopped when he noticed my tattooed arms, and I swear I saw a hint of a blush rising up his neck.

"Slade. Slade Warren." I stretched out my hand but pulled it back again when I saw all the oil, turning to grab the nearest rag I could find.

His smile had a hint of shyness now, which I didn't think suited him.

Not that I knew anything about him, but I'd read all his books. He had the skill to draw all the right emotions from a character, to the point that they felt more real to me than actual people. That said a lot to me about him.

"Let me get the keys and the invoice for you, Wren." I walked over to the office, stopping by the sink to wash my hands. I'd need to change my shirt too, but that could wait.

"How's business, Slade?" Wren asked. I handed him the invoice.

"Can't complain," I started, but then saw the smile in his eyes. "It's busy, really busy, so busy I barely even have time to take a break. I definitely don't have time to throw a ball on the football field and risk breaking my back."

He laughed and shook his head. "I'll get you one day, Slade. I'm this close to unleashing Tom on you."

I shivered. My smile turning into absolute fear.

"Please don't. I'll think about it, okay? Just give me some time to figure something out."

He smiled so wide, I threw his mom's car keys at him.

"See you later, Slade. Be gentle with my man, his clothes are very expensive."

Aiden rolled his eyes, and I watched as Wren got in his mom's car and drove off, honking the horn on his way out.

I turned to Aiden and said, "What was that about?" at the same time he said, "What did he mean?"

"You first," he said, tucking his hands in his jeans pockets. Not that I was looking or anything.

I groaned. "Tom has threatened on more than one occasion to give me a makeover. Apparently my exterior is too rough and doesn't match my soul, or some weird shit like that. I wouldn't put it past Wren to release Tom on me if I don't join the team."

"Nothing wrong with your exterior," he said and then closed his lips, catching himself.

I always imagined authors to be the kind of people who would think a lot before they spoke, as if words were so special that they needed the right kind of attention before being used. I never thought Aiden was the kind of man to let his mouth run away from him.

It was cute. Very cute.

"Speaking of exterior, give me a moment to change my shirt, or I'll be wearing this oil for real. Being a mechanic isn't as fun as Billy Joel made it look."

I could tell from the shine in his eyes that he'd stopped himself from making a comment. That, and the way he bit his lips shut.

Aiden had to be too young to know who Billy Joel was, but if he didn't get the reference he didn't show it.

Changing into a clean shirt gave me a moment to gather my thoughts.

What was he doing here? How did he know Wren? Did I make it known that I'd recognized him?

He'd said on Saturday that he was staying in town for a while, maybe his car had broken down or he was interested in buying a bike.

I ran my hands through my beard, which surprisingly had escaped the oil spill, and went back out to the garage.

Aiden was crouched by my Harley. His elbows propped on his knees and his hands supporting his head.

I'd forgotten I'd uncovered it earlier.

"It's a 1983 FXRT."

"What?" He stood and turned away from the bike.

I walked over and ran my hand over the torn leather seat. "It's a 1983 Harley-Davidson FXRT. Long-travel suspension, anti-dive front forks, stiffer frame, enclosed rear chain, and a rubber-mounted, eighty-cubic-inch Shovelhead engine. The best bike there has ever been."

"I have no idea what you just said."

Aiden stared at me with an assessing gaze. Similar to the one Wren had given me earlier, but also not.

"I'm sorry, bikes are my thing. You probably came here asking for help with your car, or something, and here I am with a bike boner the size of Texas."

He stared down at my jeans and smiled. The biting of his lips returned and, despite my inappropriate comment, I wished I could tell what he was thinking.

"Actually, I'm here for your bike knowledge."

"Okay, how can I help?"

He opened his mouth but didn't say anything, at first. In my experience, people always said exactly what they wanted when they wanted, even if they needed a little longer for the words to come out.

"I'm...um...I'm an author, and I...um, I'm doing research and need help. Wren said you could help."

His gaze veered away from me when he said he was an author, as if he were embarrassed about it. That didn't sit well with me.

"I know who you are."

"You do?"

"You seem surprised."

He put his hands in his pockets again, a gesture I was coming to understand was his way of dealing with something he wasn't comfortable with.

"No, I'm not." And then he laughed. "Sorry, actually, I am, but I know I shouldn't be."

"Oh?"

"You don't look like the kind of guy who'd read my books, although that's a terrible and judgy thought to have. Then again we met in the romance section at a book fair, so I shouldn't be surprised at all."

I smiled. "It's always a good day when you can surprise someone in a positive way." He returned my smile with his own, and his eyes were shiny with life again, more like the guy I'd met at the weekend. "So how can I help you with your research?"

AIDEN

"Are you really offering to help?" I asked.

He laughed. "You haven't yet told me what you need help with."

I pointed at the old Harley in front of us. The way he'd described all the important features of the bike told me he was absolutely the perfect person to help me with my research.

He wasn't just a subject matter expert, he was passionate about it in a way that was so captivating that I'd had to run the list of all my character names in my head to stop myself from getting a boner. And I couldn't exactly explain mine as a bike-related one, it was more a Slade-related one.

"I can tell you anything you want to know about motorcycles in general or Harleys. I've been obsessed with them since I was a kid."

"What's this bike's story?"

Slade went around the Harley, running his hand over the seat and the rusty metal arch at the back. Was that so the person riding behind had something to hold on to? I had so much to learn if I was going to make the biker in my story believable.

"This bike..." He paused, his eyes fixed on the bike and his brows furrowed. "This bike belonged to someone who meant a lot to me a long time ago."

"Does it work?"

"It's hanging by a thread. It was my passion project. I wanted to restore it to original condition, but every time I went to work on it, it didn't feel like the right time."

"And is it the right time now?"

He looked at me. His blue eyes were framed by a few wrinkles, but it only added to the broody, weathered demeanor he had going on.

"I don't know. A bike is meant to be ridden. Keeping it under a cover isn't good," he said.

"I think you should restore it. Maybe in honor of your friend, or maybe just for you, so you can drive it on your days off."

"Ride it."

"What?"

"You ride a bike, not drive it."

I sighed. "See? That's my level of understanding on this topic. I need some serious help."

He laughed, and then glanced toward the open garage door where a guy about the same height as Slade, but slimmer, came in with two coffees and two bags from Spilled Beans.

"You're a lifesaver," Slade said to the guy. "Aiden, this is Liam, he works with me."

Liam gave Slade his coffee and pastry and then shook my hand. "Pleasure to meet you. I'm really just here to do the coffee run and make sure Slade doesn't touch any cars."

I snorted and looked at Slade, who shook his head.

"Sorry, if I'd known the boss had company, I'd have brought enough for you too." Liam gave me an apologetic smile and went over to the other side of a car, where he put his coffee and pastry bag on a worktop.

Slade nodded for me to follow him inside the store. Wren and I had come in from the street straight into the garage space, so I hadn't seen the shop, other than at a glance from the other side of the glass wall.

The first thing that hit me was the smell of leather and wood. It was such a contrast from the garage, but it worked. The shop was like one of those middle-of-nowhere roadside bars. It even had some bar-like features, such as a couch and a high bar table with stools in one corner.

A photo of a bike just like Slade's hung on the wall. It was shiny and red, and I could only imagine Slade's bike would end up the same after it was restored.

"Wow, your shop looks amazing. This isn't at all how I imagined a vintage bike shop would be," I said.

Slade sat on the leather couch that was halfway between the front door and the register.

"I'm very proud of it. The whole unit, including the garage, already had the basic features I needed. The work-benches, power supply, and even the equipment. It was old but working. Where I spent more time and effort was with the shop side. I've dreamed of this space for longer than I care to remember."

He surveyed the space with a big smile on his face.

I tried not to notice the way his lips touched the coffee cup when he finally took a sip, and how his tongue poked out of his mouth a little with each sip, but that was a failed mission from the get-go.

"Is it just you and Liam?"

"Yeah, for now. I think I'm going to hire at least one other person. The car jobs are becoming more frequent, and I'd like to focus more on the bikes. I've had to turn away bike jobs to work on cars."

"Do you cry silently in the shower every time that happens?"

I pinched the bridge of my nose and let out a silent groan. Why did my mouth always run away from me when I was in this man's presence?

"Not so silently. It's more like uncontrollable sobs and very ugly crying. Not a pretty picture."

I looked at him and couldn't help laughing when I saw the teasing in his eyes. It wasn't hard to imagine Slade riding a bike, wearing a leather jacket and mirrored-lens sunglasses, his long beard with the perfect mix of silver strands through it. He'd be the perfect model for a book cover.

"So, how do you want this?"

His question brought me out of my reverie. "What?"

"How do you want to do your research?"

"Oh, um, I don't know. You're busy, so I don't want to take a lot of your time."

He ran his hand down his beard, a little lost in thought as he stared out toward the garage. Liam was surveying the tools they had hanging on the wall. Picking them and inspecting and then putting them back until he found the right one.

"The best way to learn is by doing. That's how I learned," Slade said.

"What do you mean?"

"You help me with the Harley restoration, and I tell you everything you need to know while we do it."

I laughed. "For a moment there I thought you said you wanted me to—" But his face was serious. "No...no. No! Are you insane? I'll break your bike."

He took his pastry out of the paper bag and gave it a big bite. My brain immediately forgot what we were talking about and decided to focus on the small drop of icing on his bottom lip, just where the soft-looking skin met his beard.

"Those are my terms. Come back tomorrow after five and we'll start with lesson one."

He licked his lip, catching the icing with his tongue, and then finishing the cinnamon roll in three bites.

And now I have a boner. Fan-fucking-tastic.

"What's it gonna be?"

"Do you promise I won't hurt your bike?"

Slade laughed again. His deep rumble doing nothing to make my dick get back to a disinterested state. Unlikely to happen any time I was around him. My dick was very, *very* interested.

"Don't laugh, it's a genuine concern. Do you know how many tools I own?"

His brow quirked, and a wave of heat rose up my neck. With my paler-than-vampire skin, he'd no doubt noticed the blush. Damn my parents and their genetic makeup. Couldn't I have been one of those sun-kissed kids? It wasn't for lack of holidays in the sun while growing up. But I'd never been able to tan. I was destined to look like a lobster the moment the sun so much as touched my skin.

"Why don't you tell me?"

"Huh?"

"How many...tools you own."

Go big or go home, right? "Maybe I'll show them to you one day, but I can tell you none will help fix your bike."

This time it was Slade's turn to blush. His slightly tan skin and his beard made it harder to detect any embarrassment, but there was an unmistakable twitch of his lips and shine in his eyes.

"Maybe you should go now before I decide we need lesson number one right this moment."

A shiver went up my back, and not a totally unpleasant one. His words felt like a promise, one I was absolutely certain I didn't want to accept, regardless of how much certain parts of my body wanted to.

On the other hand, my track record with men wasn't the best. Case in point, my ex who left me for another man when he figured out I had no intention of marrying him or using my family money to pay my way in life. And when I say my way, I mean his way.

No. Reading any meaning or intent into Slade's words was not the smart thing to do. I needed to just pretend I didn't see the way he looked at me, or how he seemed almost as confused about my presence as I was with his.

I stood up. "Okay. I guess I'll see you tomorrow."

His smile made the wrinkles in the corner of his eyes appear again.

Fuck my life. This was such a bad idea.

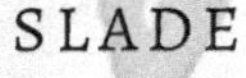

SLADE

"*H*ey, boss, I'm all done here, and I've rang Mr. Stevenson to collect his car in the morning. If you have nothing else for me, I'll head home," Liam said as I came out of the staff room.

"Thanks, Liam, that's all for today. Good job with Reed's truck."

"It's a good thing I'm not allergic to bees. I guess this one beats the sex toy catalogue I found last month."

We had a notice board in the staff room where we hung photos of all the weird stuff we found inside cars. The stranger the items were, the higher up they went on the board.

I laughed, thinking of the photo I'd taken with my phone of Liam chasing a bee around the garage and Reed chasing Liam. In the end, we managed to capture all five escaped bees and put them in a box.

Reed had a lavender farm outside town, so I was pretty sure he'd just parked his truck in the wrong spot. Bees were known to feel attracted to cars because of the warmth of the engine. Hopefully, they were now in their more natural habitat.

"I didn't think you were shutting down early today," Liam said.

"I'm not, what makes you say that?"

A smile spread on his lips.

"So you're saying you had a shower and changed into clean clothes so you can get dirty again during your lesson with the hot writer?"

I stared at him. "What? No. I stank from working all day, and I don't expect there to be much to do for the rest of the afternoon. And it's just polite to not smell like an engine when you're around other people."

He snorted. "Sure, boss. Whatever you say."

"Besides, how do you know he's hot?"

"I'm straight, boss. Not blind."

He didn't give me time to reply before he waved goodbye and ran out of the garage, saying he'd see me in the morning.

I looked at my reflection in the glass panel of my office. Did it seem like I'd made an effort?

Despite Liam's teasing, the reason I'd cleaned up before Aiden arrived was because I'd once again spilled oil all over me. Give me a bike and I was a surgeon; give me a car and I was a fucking klutz.

The phone in the office rang, but we had a cordless unit in the garage to stop us from getting our dirty hands all over the paperwork, so I walked over to the workbench and picked it up.

"Warren Automobile and Bike Repair, how can I help you?"

The chuckle from the other side made me straighten my back. "Who is this?"

"Hey, babe, it's just me."

"What do you want, Mike?"

I grabbed a wrench from the wall and squeezed it tight in my hand. The cold, hard metal a good reminder of where I was. " Why are you calling?"

My voice was steady enough, so that was good. I put the wrench back when it felt warm in my hand and picked another one.

"You put the phone down on me the other day." His voice was whiny, and it grated on me. Had he always been like this? Had I been so in love that I'd blocked it out?

"I told you I'm not interested in revisiting the past, and I'm struggling to come up with any kind of valid reason for us to be in touch."

"That's really hurtful, bab—"

"Don't call me that. Use my name and tell me what you want, or I'll hang up."

There was a brief silence on the other side.

"Why don't we speak more often, ba—Slade?"

I chose another wrench, but this time I brought it to my forehead. As ridiculous it was, the tools were actually grounding me. Or at least stopping me from blowing a gasket.

"Walking into our apartment, coming face to face with a naked twink, who looked at me as if I was the one trespassing, and then being told you were a good fuck was not, surprisingly, the highlight of our marriage."

"You said you forgave me."

His outraged tone made my blood boil.

"I took responsibility for the break in our relationship. The betrayal, the cheating, that was all on you." I hung up the call, bracing myself on the workbench.

I stared at the phone, willing it to stay silent because if it rang again, I'd need to go to the general store to buy a new one after I destroyed this one.

Maybe Mike knew it was best to stay away, or maybe having the truth slapped down the phone worked because there was no second call.

"Hey, Slade. Is this a good time? Am I too early?" Aiden asked, coming in from the street.

His smile was enough to change my mood and banish my

ex so far out of my mind, I couldn't even remember why I was holding the phone in my hand.

"Perfect timing."

"I brought you a coffee and a cookie from Spilled Beans. Figured it was the least I could do. Indy said this is how you take your coffee. Milk, no sugar."

"He's a good kid," I said, taking the coffee and cookie from Aiden. "Thank you for these. I skipped lunch."

"He's not a kid."

"Who?"

"Indy. We're the same age, and I'm definitely not a kid."

I gazed into his eyes—he'd worn his glasses again— and even from a distance I saw the challenge.

"No," I said, taking a sip of the coffee. "You're not."

"Now we've established that, how do I look?"

I spat out the coffee. Fortunately, not in his direction.

"Why do I feel that it's going to be dangerous having you around?"

He shrugged, looking down at his clothes and back to me.

The black T-shirt he had on was probably new, but his jeans...fuck me, they looked soft as butter and fit him like a glove.

"I've had these jeans since college, so I don't mind if they get ruined. And I figured I'd go for black in case I got any oil on my shirt. I hear that happens a lot here."

I'd have spat out more coffee, but after his last comment, I'd put the coffee down on the bench.

"Those are good, and we'll see how funny you are when you start getting your hands dirty. Follow me."

He chuckled but followed. The size of the garage made it easier to claim a space to work on the bike exclusively. If we were going to do this; I wanted to do it right.

"You see the tape on the floor and the wall?"

Aiden nodded.

"This means nothing that belongs to a car or another bike will ever enter this space. I know it sounds a bit much, but trust me, when you have over one hundred parts laid out on the bench or on the floor, you don't want to be guessing where they came from."

"That makes a lot of sense."

I grabbed my digital camera and handed him a notepad.

"We're going to photograph the bike, so we know exactly the state it was in originally. Everything we do will be photographed."

"Okay, what's my job, boss?"

I didn't mind when Liam called me boss, but coming from Aiden's lips it sounded wrong, unfitting.

"You write what I tell you to. This part is for your benefit. When we print out the photos, you'll be able to match them to your notes. Think of it like building a bike bible."

"Thank you, that's...really helpful. Do you not need to know what each photo is?"

"No," I said, trying but failing to keep the smugness from my voice. "I know the name of each part on this bike, down to the size of the nuts and bolts."

"Wow..." Aiden ran his hands through his hair and looked at the bike. "This is never going to work, is it?"

"What do you mean?"

"Maybe I should pick another profession for my character."

I put my hand on his arm to grab his attention.

"We need to make the most of this lighting before I shut the door. Help me with the photos, and we'll talk about that after, okay?"

Aiden nodded, still looking pensive. Yes, he could pick another profession for his character, but I'd read too many books with doctors, baristas, Navy Seals. Maybe it was stupid, but knowing there would be at least one romance novel out there with a mechanic made my profession feel visible. Like we existed not just to fix people's vehicles, but also as people who could find love. Even if only on paper.

58

AIDEN

I followed Slade around while he took hundreds of photos, but I couldn't find the excitement in it anymore.

He told me what each piece was, and I wrote it all down. Then he started removing parts from the bike and placing them neatly on the bench.

"These need to be powder-coated, we need a full engine rebuild, and—" Slade stopped and looked at me.

"Sorry, do you mind repeating that? The powder thing?"

He glanced back at the bike, and said, "You know what, let's finish for the day. We've done enough work."

"No, no, it's okay, we can carry on." I raised my notepad to show him I was ready to make more notes. "What's powder... um...thingy, anyway?"

"Powder-coating is a type of coating you apply to metals such as aluminum extrusions, drum hardware, cars, bikes, and bicycle frames. It creates a hard finish that's tougher than conventional paint."

"Okay...wait..." I wrote everything down quickly before I forgot. "Got it. Thanks."

"Aiden."

"Hmm?"

"Let's finish here. Do you want to go for a walk?"

It wasn't sunny anymore, but it was still light outside. "Sure."

I placed the notebook on the bench and waited while Slade returned the camera to his office and did the necessary checks to close the garage.

Movement from the door to the street caught my eye, but when I went to check, I didn't see anything.

"Ready?" Slade said from behind me.

"Yeah."

We slid the long metal door shut and Slade set the alarm.

"Do you live far from here?" I asked.

"I live above the shop, but there's a separate entrance."

As we walked past it, I noticed for the first time the gate to a small alleyway with a staircase at the end.

"It's nice being so close to the shop, but I miss riding to work. Where are you staying?"

"At the Old Mill."

"Oh yeah? Nice place. If the shop hadn't come with its own place, I'd have definitely considered those apartments."

The road had a curve at the end, so it wasn't until we'd gotten closer that I saw it didn't lead to another street but to a forest. A river ran between the trees and the houses, like a border to separate man from nature.

"This must be the river that runs past my apartment," I said.

We crossed the small bridge toward the forest where there was a path running alongside the river.

"That's right. We can stay on this side almost all the way to the Old Mill, then we cross again," Slade said. "If you talk to me about what was bothering you earlier, I might even buy you dinner at Benny's."

His voice was soft and low, like a caress.

I focused on the rapid flow of the water so I wouldn't have to look at Slade as I spoke.

"It's nothing big, really. My mind just went from zero to a hundred and I was overwhelmed. It happens sometimes when I can't process information in a way that makes sense. My brain is wired for storytelling. And don't get me wrong, I love research, but if I can't fit it into the story in my head, then it's like...I don't know, frustrating. "

"Which part overwhelmed you?"

A hollow laugh escaped me. "All the nuts and bolts. You mentioned all the parts and suddenly my brain realized that I'll never know enough to write a credible character."

Slade put his hand on my shoulder.

I stopped and stared at him, happy to see understanding in his blue eyes. He wasn't going to make fun of me.

"That's not true, Aiden. Do you have a medical degree? Because Doctor Misha could give me a physical any time."

I laughed at his reference to a character in one of my books.

"You should see who I used for inspiration."

"Hmm, maybe not, I'd rather imagine him in my own head. But am I right?"

I shrugged. "I guess."

"Why don't you tell me a little about your character and your story? I promise I won't share it with anyone. I don't even have a social media account."

Damn the man and his thoughtfulness.

I needed to remember that it was only acceptable to find him attractive. He was the definition of a hot silver-fox. Books should be written about how soft his beard looked, how blue his eyes were, or how the muscles in his arms moved under his white work T-shirt.

But that was it. Just because he was sweet and thoughtful didn't mean anything other than he was a decent human being.

And just because my life, until I arrived at Chester Falls, lacked in the decent human being department, it didn't mean I was going to latch on to Slade. And his sexy beard, or his arms, or...fuck.

"It's a second-chance romance between a biker and a teacher. They grow up together, then separate, meet again in their early twenties and have a fling, but something happens and they separate again. They meet ten years later when the biker has lost his husband to heart disease."

"That sounds like a great story. As long as you get the terminology right, no one will care to read the names of the parts. It's all about the love story, and that, I know for a fact, is something you excel at."

We continued walking, and I let his words sink. The path wasn't always close to the river and in some parts it went farther into the forest before winding back to the water's edge. At some point we came across a set of steps leading down to the water.

"Do people swim here in the summer?" The water flowed quite fast, but where the river wasn't as deep the sand bed beneath was visible and it didn't seem too dangerous.

"Yeah. I've seen kids jumping in and messing around, but only on really hot days."

What would it be like to use the world around you as your playground growing up? I'd lived in New York all the way until I escaped the claws of my parents' expectations and moved to San Diego. I'd traveled a lot, but I didn't remember ever feeling that free to explore the surroundings.

"You never answered my question yesterday," he said.

We crossed the bridge back to the other side, and I saw the Old Mill building and the bright neon sign for Benny's Diner.

"What question?"

"Did you read the book? I've had sleepless nights wondering."

I welcomed the change of topic as much as the warm breeze in the summer evening.

"I'm halfway. I get the reviews now."

"The ones that wish the author would slay his hands and never think a word again, let alone write it? Or the ones that think he's God's gift to literature?"

Slade wasn't wrong in his assessment of the two review camps. If that book were food, it would be pineapple on pizza.

"Hmm, I think I'll let you judge for yourself. I can give you the book at our next lesson."

Slade's grin revealed a perfect set of teeth that I was absolutely not imagining biting any part of my skin.

"Does that mean you won't give up on your story?"

I shrugged. "What can I say? This biker won't leave my mind alone."

He bumped my shoulder as we walked into Benny's.

Momma Ruth's food was, as always, amazing. How I ever survived in San Diego without this on my doorstep, I didn't know.

"What are you thinking about? You're staring at your steak as if you want to make love to it. I'm a little concerned," Slade said.

He had a crab roll and a salad, which also looked amazing.

"Are you afraid because you're going to walk home alone after dinner?" I took a bite of my steak and smiled as I chewed it.

"I am now," he said, laughing.

"I was thinking, where will I get this amazing food when I go back to San Diego."

"Is that where you're from?"

"No, I'm from New York. I moved to San Diego after college. How about you?"

He sat back and looked out the window toward the garden separating the diner and the Old Mill building. The sun was gone now, so I wondered how he'd get back home in the dark. Maybe there was a way through town.

"You know Wren from San Diego then?" Slade asked.

The avoidance of my question was as clear as if he'd written it on a piece of paper.

I leaned forward, putting my empty plate aside and crossing my arms over the table. The aluminum edge of the table was cold and dug into my arms.

"What's your story, Slade Warren?"

He smiled, but I could see it was forced. We'd only known each other a matter of days, so I had no right to press him for information. It didn't mean I wouldn't let my creative mind make something up.

I raised my hand before he spoke.

"You don't have an accent. My feeling is that this has helped you fit in everywhere you've ever been, and you've been to lots of places."

Slade's gaze cut into me, but there wasn't any anger in his eyes.

Confusion? Wonder? Maybe.

But anger? No.

I could work with that.

SLADE

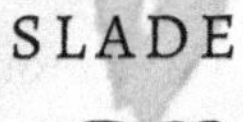

I'd met enough people in my forty-eight years that I was rarely surprised. I'd seen the best and the worst in people.

It was easy to understand people using my language. For instance, Mike was a bike. And if there was one thing I knew well, it was bikes. From the moment I'd laid eyes on him, I'd known all his parts, how each fitted into each other, and how to make the best of it.

Mike had been exactly what I'd needed at twenty-four. He didn't have a past, or anything to hide, so it had been easy to hold on to him and pretend I was like him. That there were not any ghosts chasing me. Our ride had been mostly smooth, at least I thought it had.

Aiden? Aiden was a car. It ran on the road, had an engine, breaks, and accelerator—just like a bike—except with Aiden I was a klutz, who didn't know how anything worked, as if I hadn't been around vehicles all of my life.

Four days after our dinner at Benny's, and I still had a feeling that around Aiden I'd end up with oil on my shirt more often than not.

I thought about the way he'd looked into my eyes, as if he

could see past them and locate the soul I'd sold to the devil a long time ago.

There was something about Aiden. In some ways he was a little like Mike had been when we met, but he was also so different.

I was pretty sure Aiden was a four wheels kind of guy. He was safer, had room for more people, and he could go the distance. He was definitely not the guy for me. Or the guy I deserved.

Laughter bubbled from inside me and I couldn't help but let it out. It was a good thing Liam had gone home and Aiden wasn't here yet.

Why the fuck was I thinking about Aiden?

First of all, even though I didn't know exactly how old he was, he looked like he could be my son.

Second, he was in Chester Falls only for his research and to see his friends. I knew absolutely nothing about his life in San Diego. Maybe he even had someone to go back to when he was done with me and Chester Falls.

That particular thought made my stomach churn.

Stop it, Slade.

The only mystery I wanted to solve about Aiden was why he hadn't published anything in the last year, when he was such a talented writer. And if his next book depended on the research he was doing, then I was going to do my best to help him out. End of story.

"Hey, boss, sorry I'm late."

As always, Aiden came in wearing his worn jeans and black T-shirt, except this one had NYU in washed-out writing on the front. Why did he have to be so damned sexy?

The need to get up and kiss the shit out of him to the point his glasses were all foggy and wonky on his face was too strong. I picked up a wrench and went back to the bike. Thank fuck I was sitting on a stool.

"Not your boss. I'm not paying you, remember?" I said.

"Meh, depends on what currency you trade in."

I looked up and caught him staring unashamedly at my ass.

His eyes met mine and our gazes held for a second too long.

"So, where do you want me today?" he asked, breaking the spell.

I coughed. "What?"

"Damn, you're too easy to rile up," he said, leaning against the workbench with his hands holding on to the edge.

I walked over to him, leaving only a couple of inches of separation between us.

"You know," I said, lowering my voice and whispering in his ear. "Before you rile up a biker, you should know we either ride hard or stay home."

"And...um, which one are you?"

"Take a guess..."

When I moved my head back, I saw the bob in his Adam's apple, and I'd be damned if I didn't want to take a bite.

Aiden's eyes were a dark pool, drawing me in and willing me to drown in them.

"Hello? Cover up your tools, boys."

Tom's voice coming from the door made me jump away from Aiden so fast it was as if I'd been electrocuted.

Aiden snorted, but I was already walking toward Tom, hoping the bulge in my pants would go down extra quick.

"Hey, Tom. How can I help? Car trouble?"

Tom narrowed his eyes, surveying the area as if he were trying to find something suspicious. He would have, if he hadn't announced his arrival, because I'd been half a second away from testing Aiden's lips to see if they tasted as good as they looked.

"Nope, no car trouble. I was just...um...checking in on your work."

I crossed my arms over my chest. "Oh really? I didn't know you had an interest in bikes."

He had the decency to blush a little. Tom was a firecracker at the best of times, but I hadn't met anyone more genuine and generous while also being a little, insane ball of energy in a tiny, neat package.

His outfit for the day consisted of grey slacks and a bright-yellow button-down shirt which he had paired with a burgundy fedora. Tom was a one-man runway show, making the streets of Chester Falls brighter every time he walked past. Wren was a lucky guy.

"Me? Bikes? Nah. Not interested. I just wanted to make sure Aiden wasn't wearing anything unsuitable for this kind of messy work. I couldn't live with myself if I witnessed his Tom Ford shirt get ruined and didn't do anything to stop that crime from happening."

Aiden laughed and did a full turn for Tom's benefit. "Happy?"

Tom did a big sigh and ran his hand over his forehead.

"I'm going to pretend you're not wearing university-branded cotton."

I laughed, but it soon died in my throat when Tom approached slowly, circling around me.

"Blink once if you're scared and twice if I should run for my life," Aiden said.

Tom waved a hand, coming even closer. "Pah, you already have enough style, but Slade...he's like a rough diamond. A pearl straight out of the shell. Maybe I could—"

"The only thing Slade needs is a bike between his legs."

My eyes moved to Aiden, who'd covered his mouth with both hands, as shocked with his statement as I was.

Tom grinned. If it were possible for real life sparkles to shine out of someone's eyes, Tom's gaze was the proof.

He tipped his hat before he turned around and walked

away muttering, "I hope for Wren's sake there's cupcakes at home."

I was frozen in place for a moment after Tom left, but when I finally turned to Aiden, he had his back to me and was sorting through the multiple boxes where we kept all the different small parts.

The bike engine needed to be removed today because I had someone collecting all the parts that needed painting, including the frame.

We worked in silence for a moment. Me removing as much of the small parts from the engine as I could before taking it all out, and Aiden applying WD40 to all the small pieces he bagged and labeled.

Tom's visit had caused an awkwardness to grow between us, and I didn't like that.

Aiden was usually chatty as he worked. He'd told me that when he's writing, he needed complete silence, but if he was doing something with his hands, he just couldn't keep his mouth shut.

His words had created a back and forth of comments between us. Just one of the many times we'd flirted all week. I couldn't explain it, but we'd found a rhythm of working and teasing each other that made the evenings go fast too quickly.

I found myself wishing every day away so the afternoon would come and it would be time for Aiden. And most evenings this week, we'd ended up having dinner together at Benny's.

"Can you give me a hand?" I asked, hoping I could gauge his mood if he was actually facing me.

"Sure."

I explained where he needed to hold the engine while I worked on the last few bolts.

"That's it...nearly there."

With the engine out of the frame, we packed up for the evening.

"Slade?"

"Yeah?"

Aiden cleaned his hands on a rag and looked at the empty frame of the bike.

"How does it feel? Riding a bike?"

I smiled. Riding a bike was like staring into Aiden's eyes. It was scary and exhilarating, pleasure and anxiety.

"Riding a bike is...life, Aiden. It's the scariest thing you can do, but also the most freeing. When you're on a bike, it's just you, the power between your legs, and the road. There are no expectations, no judgement, no history, no past. Sometimes there's no future, but you always have somewhere to go. The destination rarely matters, it's the journey that makes the difference."

I didn't realize Aiden had come closer until his arms wrapped around my waist and I was enveloped in a pine-scented hug.

My heart beat so fast that I wondered if I was at an age where I needed to see the doctor for it, but I knew it was all Aiden. He was the one bringing out all the feelings I mostly shied away from.

"Thank you," I said.

"What? No, I'm the one who needs to thank you for sharing that with me." He stepped away from my embrace and put his hands in the pockets of his jeans.

It was such an adorably Aiden gesture.

"Are you doing anything on Sunday?" I asked.

"Not particularly. Do you want to work on the engine? I've been reading the manual. You can test me on it."

That was another uniquely Aiden trait. Despite his initial lack of confidence about the challenge of rebuilding the bike, he'd made it his job to learn everything he could.

"Not quite. Meet me outside at ten on Sunday morning."

"Okay, what are we doing?"

"You'll see."

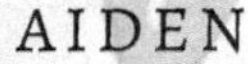

*I*t didn't matter that I'd had a whole day before my date with Slade.

I ran through all my clothing options and still came up short on what to wear. If it wasn't for the certain inquisition I'd get from Tom about this supposed date, I'd have called for his help.

And I definitely did not need anyone else to blow this out of proportion.

I was doing that very well on my own, considering in my head I'd been calling this a date.

A date.

Just because he said we wouldn't be working on the bike.

Just because it was Sunday didn't mean this was a date.

And just because we nearly kissed before Tom interrupted us, it didn't mean Slade wanted to kiss me. At all. No matter how much I wanted to kiss him.

I'd spent the whole week sneaking peeks at him while we worked. I just couldn't help myself.

Slade was unlike any man I'd met before.

On the outside, he had this bad-boy biker look going on. I'd noticed the tattoos that peeked from under the short sleeves of his work shirts and wondered if he had them only on his arms or elsewhere on his body.

His hair was a perfect mix of grey and white, shorter on the sides and back and longer on top, and then there was his long beard. Richard had always had a close shave, so I'd never considered how I might enjoy or appreciate facial hair on other men.

Slade was also kind and patient. Even after a whole day at work, he still had time for all my questions. He seemed to be going through the process of breaking the bike into its several parts, with the joy of a child playing with their favorite new toy on Christmas morning.

There was only one topic he'd avoided. Every time I mentioned motorcycle clubs, he changed the subject. He was nice about it, but I could tell it wasn't something he wanted to talk about.

Which, of course, meant I was even more curious about it, and him.

I arrived at his gate with five minutes to spare. My heart was beating so fast I thought I was going to pass out. Dammit, I should have had more than half a bagel for breakfast.

The big metal door to the garage was closed, as was the gate to the alleyway to Slade's place.

I couldn't see a bell either, but since we agreed to meet at ten, I figured he'd be down soon, so I sat on the concrete step outside.

More thoughts of Slade filled my head. Whatever the day brought, I was really excited to be spending more time with him. My new daily routine consisted of writing in the morning followed by research while I tried to not arrive at the garage so early that I'd come across as overly keen.

I was so lost in thought that when I felt a bump against my back, I jumped up from the step.

"What the—"

A kitten was on the other side of the gate, sitting on its back legs and staring at me.

"Hello, you. Was I in your way?"

I crouched to his level, thinking he'd probably scoot off to his home, but he just stood there roaring at me. He had a beautiful ginger coat and green eyes, but he was so small that he couldn't be an adult yet.

"Are you lost?"

He replied with another tiny roar.

"You have quite a big roar for such a little kitten," I said, reaching out to him slowly. "I hope you're not lost, buddy."

He stretched out his neck to meet my hand and bumped his head against my fingers. I turned my hand slowly to pet him, but suddenly he ran back toward the alleyway.

A minute later I saw Slade come down the stairs at the end of the alleyway holding a bunch of stuff.

"Hey. Sorry, I realized too late that you didn't have my number and there's no doorbell. I hope you weren't waiting long."

My brain struggled to form words at the sight of Slade in black jeans, a white T-shirt, and a leather jacket.

"No, not waiting long...um, just got...here. What have you got there?"

"This jacket is for you to wear and this is your helmet," he said.

"My what?"

He chuckled. "Hold these, I'll be right back.

When my brain caught up, I laughed to myself. Surely he didn't mean—

"He fucking did."

Fortunately, he didn't hear me over the noise of the big, badass bike.

I was still staring at him when he parked the bike to close the gate. Was that the right term? Do bikes get parked? Or is it a different term?

Slade appeared in my line of sight.

"You look a little terrified... Okay, a lot. You don't have to do this, but I thought it would be fun for you to experience what it's like to ride on a bike."

"I am...terrified." The bike was big and sturdy. Newer than the one we were working on, but still a Harley. Still only two wheels.

Before I could change my mind, I gave him my helmet so I could put the jacket on. It was surprisingly light. Then I put the helmet on my head but couldn't figure out how to fasten it.

"Here. Let me do it," Slade said, taking over with the expertise of someone who'd done it a million times. I tried to ignore the little sparks I felt when his fingers brushed against my skin.

He put his helmet on and straddled the bike.

"Damn."

"What's up?"

"Do you have a pair of sunglasses?" I asked.

"Yes."

"Put them on."

He raised a brow but did as I asked.

I took my phone out of my pocket and snapped a photo.

"Thank you, god. I'll never ask for anything ever again," I said to myself, pocketing the phone.

"My name's Slade, and those who don't ask, never get."

His teasing smile was what wet dreams were made of.

"I think I need a cold shower," I muttered as I tried to get on the bike behind him in the most gracious way I could. Mission failed.

"Maybe later, if you're good," he said.

"Damn it, Slade, if you're gonna look like my teenage fantasy and talk like it too, you better come through."

He laughed and told me to hold on tight.

I kept my eyes closed to start with because I was terrified

that if I opened them, I'd throw up from fear. Especially as Slade navigated the tight streets of Chester Falls.

When it seemed we were on a straight road, I loosened my grip around Slade and opened my eyes.

Everywhere around us was green. Green fields, pastures, hills. It was beautiful. The rumble of the bike was loud, but after a while, I got used to it and it became almost soothing. I didn't realize how smooth it could be to ride a bike.

I didn't know how long or far we traveled because at some point Slade put his hand over mine and left it there. I leaned my head against his back and just enjoyed the ride.

We occasionally traveled through towns, but mostly through the countryside. I stopped trying to make sense of our destination or direction until Slade took a turn to a small track and stopped the bike under the shade of a tree.

My legs were shaking with adrenaline when I came off the bike, so I sat on a patch of grass nearby. We were in some kind of forest, but the trees were spaced enough apart that sunlight still came through the branches.

Slade took my helmet and his and hung them on the handles of the bike. Then he sat next to me.

His eyes had never looked so blue before, his smile so candid. He had never looked so free.

Maybe it was the adrenaline still rushing through my veins, but before I could think too much about it, I straddled Slade and pressed my lips against his.

His hand came up to rest on the back of my neck to keep me exactly where I was. As if I had any intention of going anywhere.

Slade's lips were ridiculously soft and his beard was a little rough against my skin, which only served to make the kiss a thousand percent hotter.

I wanted his mouth everywhere on me; I wanted his beard to scratch me head to toe.

Breathing was so overrated. Who needed to draw a breath when we could live on each other's taste forever?

I deepened the kiss, running my tongue over his lips and sucking them into my mouth, first the top one and then I dragged my teeth over his bottom one, pulling it.

Slade let out what sounded like a growl and flipped us around so he was on top of me.

The squeaky sound of his leather jacket, how he owned my mouth, the way his bigger body was heavy on top of me...I needed more and I needed less. Less clothes, more Slade.

This was getting out of control. Would taking this farther be taking it too far?

When Slade stopped the kiss, leaning his forehead on mine, we were both breathless.

I stared into his eyes and they were no longer blue. They were as dark as night, and I'd be damned if I didn't want a sleepover.

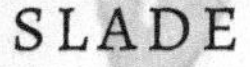
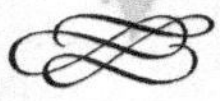

"Aiden," I whispered, still trying to control my breathing and my raging hard-on.

He placed his hands on either side of my face. They were soft, and I couldn't help turning to kiss one palm and then the other.

"Don't say we shouldn't." His voice was low. As though if the world around us discovered what we'd done maybe it would start meaning something.

I nodded, but I knew we shouldn't. Aiden was too young, too good for me, and I could never be the person he deserved.

Not that it had stopped me from claiming him like a wild animal.

Once his lips had touched mine and he'd ran his fingers through my hair, pulling it so tight my scalp still hurt, I would have had to be a saint to be able to resist Aiden.

And one thing I knew for sure, I'd never claimed to be a saint. Quite the opposite.

The thought that he'd gotten as lost in the kiss as I had, made me feel like a man half my age. I couldn't remember the last time I'd kissed like that, the last time I had been kissed like that.

"Why did you bring me here?" he asked.

I stared into his big, brown eyes. He'd worn his contacts, so I could see from this close how beautiful his eyes were, so deep, with a dark-blue ring around the iris.

To prove to myself I really wasn't a saint, or maybe that I'd just lost all self-control around Aiden, I kissed him one last time before standing on my knees and bringing him up with me.

Even though this was a fairly unknown spot—something I'd assumed from the lack of seeing anyone else around whenever I came here—I made sure the bike was locked properly.

I took the two helmets from the handle and told Aiden to follow me. We didn't have to walk farther than a hundred yards to get to the spot I wanted to show Aiden.

We were on higher ground, looking into the valley below.

This was my thinking place. It was peaceful and undisturbed.

Coming here served as a reminder of how lucky I'd been. Still was. My fate could have been so different if I'd carried on the destructive path of my youth.

When I was here, I knew I'd made at least one good decision in my life.

"Wow, is that lavender?" Aiden asked as soon as we got to the top of the small incline.

"Yes. That's Reed's farm."

"Reed... Isn't that where Indy and Tate got married?"

"Yeah." Most of the time I'd spent with Aiden was just us, so I'd forgotten he knew the guys due to being friends with Wren.

"I thought we were farther away from Chester Falls. Isn't Reed's farm only half an hour away from town?" he asked.

"Yeah, we're quite close. We went in a big circle to give you the riding experience, but I wanted to bring you here."

Aiden closed his eyes and inhaled the lavender-infused breeze.

I wanted to put my arms around him, inhale his scent, and lick that spot of exposed skin between the collar of his shirt and his hairline.

In the sunlight his skin was even more perfect. So white, smooth, soft. I imagined Aiden wasn't the kind of man to mark his skin with tattoos. Not that there was anything wrong with tattoos. I had plenty and liked them, but the thought of exploring Aiden's unmarked skin made me lightheaded.

"Slade."

"What?"

"You're looking at me like you want to eat me. Should I be worried?"

I scratched my beard and ran my fingers down to straighten it. Aiden's eyes followed my hand as if he wanted to do it himself.

"Only if you have issues being mauled by an old man with very little self-restraint around you."

He turned his back on the view to face me and ran his hands up my chest slowly before grabbing on to the collar of my jacket.

"First of all, you're not old—"

"I'm forty-eight."

"Thank you for telling me, but I don't care about your age. I'm thirty, by the way, so you're not exactly cradle snatching."

I smiled.

"And second, I am very up for being mauled."

"Oh, Aiden..." I let my words hang because I didn't know what else to say. This man was something else. "How about we grab some lunch? There's a place not far from here. They do good food."

"Sounds excellent."

The roadside diner wasn't as busy as I'd seen it before, maybe because it was still a little early for lunch, so instead of sitting at the bar, I led us to a booth.

"Do you do this often?" he asked.

"I try to ride on Sundays. There aren't as many tractors on the roads that I like to take."

"When did you start riding?"

The waitress came to take our order, so I waited until she was gone.

"I was fourteen. The guy living next door to my foster parents had a bike and was always working on it. He'd leave his garage door open. There wasn't much to do outside of school, and my parents couldn't afford to send us to after-school classes or do sports, so I started hanging out with him. When I turned fifteen, I got my learner's permit and he taught me everything he knew."

"I can imagine you as a little kid, hovering over the biker dude, asking a million questions, and dying to ride a bike."

I laughed. "How do you do that?"

"Do what?"

"How do you know...me?"

I wasn't sure I wanted him to answer the question, but it was the second time he'd assessed me correctly, as if he'd been there all my life.

He shrugged. "It's all written in your eyes. You just need to learn how to decode it."

Our food came—putting an effective stop to our conversation—piping hot and looking as delicious as every other meal I'd had on the few occasions I'd stopped there.

"Oh my god, this is amazing. Jesus, between this place and Benny's, I'm seriously considering moving to Chester Falls."

I examined his expression to see if there was any real truth or intention in his statement, but Aiden was focused on dipping chunks of the homemade sourdough into his soup.

Would he really consider moving to Chester Falls? As an author, I guessed he could work anywhere, but since he'd already moved from New York to the west coast, maybe he didn't want to move back east again.

And why was I thinking about it as if it could happen?

The waitress came over to refill our coffee.

"Can I interest you in a slice of pie?" she asked. "Today's special is my great-grandma's cherry pie."

Aiden's face lit up. "Is it really?"

"Nah, I got the recipe off the internet, but I can tell you it's better than my great-grandma's pie. Legend goes that she was a terrible cook."

"Two slices please," I said. "And can you put two more in a box to go?"

"Sure thing, Daddy."

Aiden was struggling to keep a straight face after the waitress left.

"Um...anything you want to share...Daddy?"

There was a glint in his eyes. I liked that. I liked that a lot.

"Look around. The girl can't be older than twenty. Half the men here are old enough to be her dad."

"Uh huh, if you say so...Daddy." The way he said the word as he held my gaze under his spell was enough to get my dick hard again.

I wasn't into Daddy kink, or that kind of role play, but I had a feeling I'd be into anything with Aiden if he ever asked for it.

He chuckled. "You are a lot more transparent than you think, Slade Warren."

"While you are still a mystery to me, Aiden Lawton."

"I'm anything but a mystery. In fact, a few google searches will tell you anything you need to know."

Despite his smile, and how casual he tried to sound, I still detected a hint of unease.

"I can guarantee that what I want to know about you can't be found on an internet search," I said, reaching out for his hand over the table.

He gave it to me, no questions asked. I ran my thumb over his knuckles before drawing circles over the back of his hand.

"Aiden, I need you to know I wouldn't look you up and

invade your privacy like that. Not even before I met you." He nodded and a small smile graced his lips. "But if you tell me there's a sex tape out there, then I have a cupboard full of popcorn at home."

A piece of bread flew in my direction, but I was quick enough to catch it midair and stop it from hitting anyone sitting behind me.

I put the bread in my mouth and grinned.

"You're an animal," he said.

I winked at him. "About that sex tape..."

He bit his lip.

Fuck.

AIDEN

Of course there was no sex tape. Not that Richard hadn't asked on multiple occasions if we could tape ourselves having sex, but I'd always said no.

It didn't mean I couldn't tease Slade though, but a group of men walking in the diner got my attention.

"Oh my god, Slade, are those real-life bikers?"

He looked behind him to the door where the men wearing leather vests with patches sewn on them had grouped by the bar. The waitress pointed toward a booth on the far side of the diner and they all followed the guy that came in first.

"Do you think they'd be willing to talk to me?"

"No!"

Slade's answer was so abrupt that I turned my gaze from the bikers to him.

"Why?" I frowned and crossed my arms.

So far he'd avoided all my questions about bikers. Anything about motorcycles he'd spell out the equivalent to a ten-page essay for the smallest question. When I wanted to know about bikers, he clammed up.

Well, I had a book to write, and my career was on the line, so if he couldn't help me, then I'd find someone who could.

"You don't want to mess with bikers, Aiden."

His tone was so unyielding it was getting on my nerves. I was tired of half-answers.

"Why? Because they're dangerous?"

"Yes."

"Are you saying that all bikers are dangerous? Because that's incredibly judgmental. I don't want to know what activities they get involved in. I want to know how they function as a unit, how do they find each other, and how they decide who's in and who's out."

He looked behind him again. One of the bikers was back at the bar talking to the waitress. They seemed friendly enough. I tried to read the patch on the back of his vest.

The letters were too close together, but I could make out *The Lost Puppies*, and then under a logo, which looked like a dog, it had *Connecticut*. A motorcycle club named The Lost Puppies couldn't be all that dangerous, could it?

"Aiden," Slade's voice was calm, but I could detect the underlying unease. "Biker clubs *earned* their reputation. Think about that. Can't you find what you need for your book on the internet?"

"No."

"Fine." He got up from the booth and put some money on the table. "Go talk to them and come find me when you're done." Then he turned around and left.

What the fuck?

My blood that had been simmering under the surface came to a boil. I took the money to the bar and gave it to the waitress. She tried to give me the pie slices, but I couldn't think of anything food related right now. I told her to keep the pie money as a tip.

Slade wasn't by his bike, so I walked around and saw a path leading to an empty kids' playground. I found him sitting on the back of a bench on the other side.

"Got what you need?" he asked, standing up and not looking at me.

"Of course not, you dumbass."

He raised his eyes to meet mine.

"Do you think I was going to approach a group of men I don't know to ask them those kinds of questions just like that? Do you think I'm that stupid? Especially after you warned me?"

His shoulders sagged a little, but I wasn't backing down. I needed an explanation.

"I take it they're not that dangerous, considering you walked out knowing there was a possibility I might approach them."

The twitch of his lip told me I was right.

"Dammit, Aiden, what do you want?"

I went over to him and put my hands on his jacket, forcing him to look me in the eye.

"Would they have answered my questions?"

"No."

"Why?"

"Because they have a code of conduct and you're not part of them."

"And how do you know that?"

His eyes left mine briefly before they returned full of pain.

"Because I used to be one of them."

The statement didn't surprise me. The fact he didn't want to talk about it made me wonder how much he really knew about motorcycle clubs and why he didn't seem to be in one.

"You used to be in that club?" I asked.

"No, not that one." He took a deep breath. The wrinkles around his eyes suddenly seemed deeper. "It was a long time ago, Aiden. It's a part of my life that I don't want to remember. I did things I'm not proud of. But it's in the past. I've already shared with you more than I ever shared with anyone else. Doesn't that count for something?"

I went on my tiptoes—because the man was a freaking giant—and kissed him. He relaxed and allowed me to deepen the kiss.

When his arms went around me, I knew we were okay... well, sort of.

"Slade, I don't want you to ever do anything that is painful to you. I know this might seem like just a book to you, but this is the most important thing I have in my life right now. I need to make it right."

He nodded. "Maybe I can help you." I smiled and was going to thank him when he put his finger over my lips. "I can't promise I'll be able to answer all your questions, but I'll try."

"Okay."

"In return I need you to make me a promise."

"Okay."

"If there is something I can't tell you, it's because it could put your safety in jeopardy. It means you can't go ask anyone else, especially not random bikers you might find at roadside diners."

"I promise," I said.

"Just like that?"

"Just like that."

Whatever was in his past was in his past. Maybe he'd done stupid or dangerous stuff, but I trusted him.

When we got back to the bike, he helped me put my helmet on. I wasn't stupid enough to admit I'd figured out how to do it on my own. Having Slade's hands on me beat not having them on me any day.

He put his own helmet on and then grabbed my hand and placed the keys to the bike in my palm.

A rush of excitement and nerves went up my spine. "Are you serious?"

"A little bit too much sometimes, or so I'm told," he replied.

I went to punch his shoulder, but he anticipated my move and wrapped his arm around my waist. The rush that went up my spine turned into lust when he nuzzled my neck and sucked my exposed skin.

"I bet you're gonna look so hot riding that bike," he said into my ear, just before he sucked my lobe.

"I won't be able to drive if my brain is a puddle of mush by our feet. Keep doing that, and I'll forget how to walk, let alone drive this thing," I said. I didn't move away from his touch though.

It felt so damned good, and I was not a stupid man. Well, not always.

"Ride it, Aiden. You're gonna ride it."

"I fucking hope so," I muttered to myself and forced a separation before I did something that would give the people in the bar a show and us arrested.

He chuckled and pointed to the bike.

I straddled it first and he got on behind me.

"Okay, what do I do?"

"First you need to unlock the bike. Put the key in the fork lock right over there." He pointed to the side of the bike under the handle.

The bike wobbled a little when I unlocked it, but Slade put his hand on the handle to keep it steady. My hands shook from nerves.

"I'm going to crash."

Slade laughed.

"I hope you enjoyed your time on this planet. Did you ever think you'd die at the hands of your favorite author?"

He turned my head around to face him and kissed me senseless.

"I can think of worse ways to go than on a bike with my all-time favorite author, but we're not gonna die. At least not before you have a chance to ride me."

I groaned. "Fuck me, Slade."

"I plan to, baby. Now stop freaking out. I'm here to help you."

"Wait," I said, "Are you saying that to distract me?"

He traced my lips with his thumb, and then groaned when I opened my mouth and licked it. "It's really not in my best interests to have you distracted, Aiden. I can ride if you're too anxious."

I turned around and steadied myself. "Nope, I'm doing this."

"Okay, open the door on the ignition switch, put the key in, and turn it to the right."

I jumped when the bike started and felt Slade laughing behind me. I'd have elbowed him, but I was too scared of what was coming to focus on payback. He'd have that later, with a cherry on top.

And by cherry, I meant me.

Slade's height proved useful because he was tall enough to reach the side of my head and talk to me. He also helped me to get going by showing me how to use the handles and the brakes. It was a little weird at first, but as soon as we got on the road, it was much easier, and I found my own stride.

"Woohoo!" I shouted. "Let's get home and get naked!"

Oops, did I say that aloud?

SLADE

Okay, I was officially impressed. Not only had Aiden learned how to ride the bike in no time at all, but he also seemed to be a natural.

Curves were tricky for a beginner, and I'd been ready to help him, but he seemed to have figured it out all on his own.

Not that the road to Chester Falls was particularly challenging, but damn, I was so proud of him.

I was also fucking hard to the point of being painful.

We had to contend with the town traffic, but forty minutes after leaving the roadside bar, we were pulling up at the Old Mill.

Despite having openly flirted with Aiden, I didn't want to make assumptions. Hell, flirting wasn't even it. I'd categorically said I wanted to fuck him.

He'd been partially correct, I was trying to distract him. It just so happened I was also telling the truth. After that first kiss, I knew there was no way I could resist Aiden. If he was up for some fun, I wasn't going to say no.

When Aiden stopped the bike, I helped him turn it off and lock it.

He removed his helmet and ran his hand over his hair

before turning his head around. His eyes were filled with anticipation, heat, and uncertainty.

"Um...do you want...would you like...um, do you want to come up for a coffee?"

I smiled and removed my own helmet. "I'd love to."

We walked silently side by side to the main entrance of the building.

Ollie, the town gardener, was on the lawn in front of the building watering the flowers while barefoot.

"Hey, Ollie, how's it going?" I asked when he waved.

"Good, good. Always good when the sun is shining and the flowers are thirsty. Growing takes a lot of effort," he said.

"You're preaching to the choir, Ollie."

He turned his head sideways, his gaze going between me and Aiden. "Mmhmm, I don't know, sometimes growing can be a lot of fun too."

He reached out to a box he had nearby and took out a small bag. "Here you go. Plant these in a pot by your window. They're tough little plants, so even if they don't get lots of attention growing up, they always seem to shine through in the end."

I took the bag from Ollie, unsure of what to say.

He waved us off and we waved back. Ollie was a funny old character. No one was quite sure how old he was because with every conversation he always imparted some bite of wisdom, but he also looked weirdly youthful. Maybe that was what working with nature did to you.

I followed Aiden through the main door of the building and into the elevator. Throughout the ride up, he kept moving his weight from one foot to the other.

Everyone knew coffee didn't really mean coffee, but what if he *really* meant coffee and now he wondered if I thought we were having coffee or having *coffee*?

I hadn't been with someone in such a long time that I'd

forgotten all the rules. To be honest, I'd never played by any rules because I'd never played.

With Mike I'd been straight with him from the get-go. I'd told him that if we were working together and fucking, he'd better tell his uncle. I'd expected him to back off before anything started, but my straight forwardness only spurred him on.

After Mike, I'd only been with a handful of men. Not quite hookups, but also not quite relationships. And I'd been as open with them as I'd been with Mike.

I followed Aiden down a long corridor, appreciating the architecture of what had been left from the old textiles mill that gave the building its name.

Aiden stopped so suddenly that I nearly bumped into him.

"I don't want coffee," he blurted out.

"Okay."

His eyes were wide and his breathing was coming in short bursts, as if he couldn't quite believe what he'd just said. He stared straight ahead, which meant he was staring right at my chest.

"So...no caffeinated drinks," I said.

He nodded.

It didn't take more than a small move to have him against the wall. I braced against it with one hand and ran the other gently up his neck, caressing his sharp jaw and tilting his head up.

"Maybe soda?" I teased.

He shook his head.

I didn't know where this shy Aiden had come from all of a sudden, but he was fucking adorable. Still sexy as hell though. But there was no way we'd do anything he didn't want or wasn't ready for.

"Cake?"

He shook his head again. "No cake."

"Damn, I didn't even get pie earlier."

Aiden's brown eyes darkened and a smile teased his lips.

"Where's the Aiden that wanted to ride me?"

"He abandoned me."

"Oh really?" I took his hand in mine and laced our fingers. "Is this the hand that commanded my bike so perfectly? That knew when to brake smoothly or accelerate?"

He nodded.

I kissed his hand, and then using my knee, I coaxed him to spread his feet wider, wedging my thigh between his legs. His hardness gave me the confidence to carry on.

"Are those the thighs that kept us stable on the straight road and made the bike hug each curve?"

He closed his eyes. His mouth parted slightly as he leaned his head back against the wall.

I wanted to suck on that perfect skin, kiss those lips I now knew to be softer than cotton candy and just as sweet.

"Then, *that* Aiden is here. The question is... Does he still want me?"

"All the Aidens want you, Slade," his voice was almost a whisper.

A cough made me jump away from Aiden, although I didn't know why I bothered because there was no way to explain why we were basically eye-fucking against a wall.

"Tristan...hi," Aiden said.

I never thought it was possible for someone to go that red, but Aiden managed it just by looking at Tristan's all-knowing smile.

"So..." Tristan said, pointing at both of us. "I like it. I really like it. Now, I know you don't need the talk about the birds and the bees, so you're off the hook."

He scratched his hair, pretending to think carefully about his next words.

"I'll give you a free full car service if you wait at least

twenty-four hours until you tell anyone what you saw here," I said.

"Twenty-four hours?" Aiden screeched.

"Aid, there's a five hundred percent chance he snapped a photo of us and sent it to Ben before he gave his presence away."

Aiden's chin fell, and I wasn't sure if it was because of me openly giving him a nickname or because, from the expression on Tristan's face, I'd been right on the money.

"I guess it's only fair. You're lucky I'm not married to Tom, or you'd have your wedding planned and your children's names picked by now. As you were..."

Tristan walked down the corridor and pressed the elevator button. Since we'd just gotten off of it, the doors opened straight away. He wedged his foot to keep them open and said, "Oh, you might want to accept the invite to come out with the guys on Friday."

"What does he mean?" Aiden asked. "Wait, let's go into the apartment before we have any more weird encounters."

I followed him inside. Aiden had said he was renting the apartment from someone who was away, so that accounted for all the elements that made the place feel really homey, but it was all the papers, notepads, and laptop on the dining table that made the place Aiden's.

"Do you want a drink?" he asked.

"I thought you didn't have any drinks available." I put my hands in my jeans pockets, mirroring him. He was going to have to make the first move if he wanted anything to happen between us, but I'd be damned if I wasn't going to show how much I really wanted him.

He looked at my growing bulge and walked toward me. With one hand he pushed me backward until the backs of my legs touched the couch.

I sat down and was surprised when Aiden straddled me for the second time that day.

If he was going to make a habit of this, I'd need to invest in sweatpants. Easier access and more room to move.

Aiden rested his hands on my chest and sat back on my legs.

"About Tristan..."

"What about him?" I asked.

"Is he really going to tell everyone he saw us?"

I tried to see in Aiden's expression if this was something that worried him. I understood that it could be an issue because he wasn't exactly an unknown person.

"He was mostly teasing, but he won't tell anyone if we ask him," I reassured him.

"Would it bother you if they knew?"

I chuckled. "I'm too old to care about what people think."

"There you go again with the age thing. Do you have a problem with your age? Because I resent that on your behalf."

"How noble of you. My fragile ego thanks you."

His eyes scanned me from my head to my crotch. "There's nothing fragile about you."

"So you don't mind if they know who you're sleeping with?"

Aiden came so close that I felt his breath on my lips. "Who said anything about sleeping?"

He slammed his mouth against mine, which was when I gave myself permission to touch him.

Fucking finally.

"Jesus. Fuck, Aiden. You're going to kill me with how fucking sexy you are," I growled against his lips.

"Shh, no dying. I'm not done riding for the day."

AIDEN

I felt like we'd been engaging in the longest foreplay in history since that first kiss this morning, and oh my sweet lord, what a kiss that was.

Slade's mouth was commanding, demanding, sweet, and tender. How did he set my body on fire with just one kiss?

So yeah, I was desperate for more, and I wasn't waiting another second for it.

I pulled away from Slade's mouth— using self-restraint that should earn me some kind of award—and tried to stand up, but he put his hands on my thighs.

"Where are you going?"

"Unless you have a self-lubricating dick, we're gonna need supplies," I chuckled.

He pulled me in for another kiss, biting my tongue gently before letting go. "I love your smart, sassy mouth, Aiden Lawton."

"You better have lost those jeans by the time I'm back...oh, and leave the jacket on."

I ran to the bathroom attached to the bedroom. When I opened my washbag, I realized that my condoms could well be out of date. I'd bought them as an act of rebellion after my relationship with Richard ended but hadn't actually used them.

Fuck, fuckity, fucks.

I turned one over, letting out a *fuck yes*, when I saw it was still good, then grabbed the bottle of lube from the bedroom and ran back to the living room.

My throat closed up at the sight of Slade almost fully naked on the couch, wearing just the leather jacket, a pair of red boxer shorts, and tattoos that definitely went beyond what I'd seen on his arms.

"Fuck my life, Slade, you're...fuck."

"I'm naked, that's what I am. And you're not."

I threw the supplies onto the couch next to Slade and started by taking my shoes off, nearly keeling over in the process.

"Slowly, Aid. I want to watch as you reveal your milky white skin to me."

"You mean pasty," I said. I'd always been quite self-conscious that I couldn't get a tan and now, facing a very naked Slade with his tan complexion and tattoos, I realized we couldn't be more different than a car and a bike.

He stood up and pulled me by the hand to come closer. "I've been wanting to see you naked since you stole that book from me—"

"Hey," I tried to argue, but he laughed and took my distraction as an opportunity to lift my shirt over my arms.

"As I suspected, you're perfect."

I traced the tattoos on his chest. There were so many that I'd need a lifetime to explore them all to my satisfaction. The thought gave me butterflies in my stomach. What the hell was I thinking? This was just sex between two people who clearly were extremely attracted to each other.

It was time to take control and stop the mushy thoughts.

I pushed Slade back onto the couch and he landed with a

thump. Then I finished undressing until I was fully naked in front of Slade.

His eyes zeroed in on my cock and he wet his lips. I stroked my length, running my thumb over the crown and picking up a bead of precum.

Slade's eyes went impossibly dark when I raised my thumb to my mouth. "You want it?"

"Yes." His voice was breathy.

I kneeled between his legs and fed him my thumb, which he licked and sucked on as if it were my dick. I treated it as a promise, but not for that moment because I needed him inside me, stat.

"I never pinned you for a red underwear man," I said, running my hands up his thighs until the tips of my fingers ghosted over his erection.

He hissed. "Oh yeah? What did you pin me as?"

"Someone who likes to take control, but you'll give it up for the right man. Someone who isn't afraid to be himself. You're dark, sexy leather, but sometimes you're soft, silky satin."

I bent down to kiss his cock over his underwear. My mouth watered at the thought of sucking him and hearing him moan under my touch.

"Aid." His voice was raspy and full of need. Wren was the only person that had ever called me Aid, but the nickname coming from Slade's lips sounded so different. It was like a prayer only I could answer.

I pulled his boxer shorts down and under his ass until they were gone. His cock was thick and long, framed by a trimmed thatch of grey hair. I hoped he didn't mind that other than shaving my balls, I didn't trim my pubic hair.

His cock was heavy in my hand, like a satin-covered rod of steel. I cringed at my own thoughts, but once a romance author, always a romance author. And Slade's cock was very much romance-novel worthy.

"Are you going to suck it or write stories in your head about it?"'"

I looked up at him.

"I'm not the only one who's easy to read, Aid." He ran his hand over my head, gently. "And I definitely want to know what that dirty little mind of yours was thinking, but I'll get a complex if you don't actually—"

His words got stuck in his throat at the same time his cock went deep into mine. Because, apparently, I'd decided I had no gag reflex and wanted Slade's dick in my mouth so much that I couldn't wait to find out if I could fit it all in.

I couldn't. Of course, I couldn't. His romance-novel-worthy cock was too big, but fuck it felt amazing in my mouth. If only it were possible to have it in my mouth and get fucked by it at the same time.

"Aid, fuck...stop."

As soon as I released him, he pulled me up on his lap so I was straddling him again and kissed me until I failed to remember my name.

"What's wrong?" I asked.

"You were in another world. Jesus, Aid. I nearly blew in your mouth."

"You make it sound like it's a bad thing," I said.

"It is if you still want to...you know. My recovery time isn't what it used to be."

There was no way I'd tell him what I had in mind when I was sucking him, but the thought he nearly lost it made me hot all over.

He took a deep, steadying breath and ran his hands over my chest and down my belly until they reached my cock.

"God, you're so beautiful, Aiden."

"Says the sex-on-legs, hot silver-fox biker."

"You seem to have a thing for bikers," he said.

"I do now."

I rolled the condom down his length and added some lube to it. Then I ran a lubed finger over my hole.

Slade held me up. One of his hands stroked my length, while the other followed my hand as I prepped.

"Need to make sure you're ready," he said.

"I'm ready." I raised myself up on my knees and lined his cock with my hole.

"Aiden, that wasn't enough."

"Trust me, it's enough. I'm already stretched."

I felt my skin heat up even as I said the words, so I replaced the awkwardness of having to admit to using my toys while thinking of him, with something better.

"Fuck, you're so thick. Make me feel so full," I groaned as inch-by-inch Slade filled me. He was so hard and hot inside me that I needed to be careful or I'd come as soon as I moved.

My cock was hard and leaking between us.

I took Slade's mouth and kissed him with all I had while I held on to his hair. Only by distracting myself with his mouth would I be able to move again without setting off my orgasm.

Had it been so long since I'd had sex that my body was ready to explode in just a minute? Or was it because Slade was just so good?

"Jesus Christ, Aid. Ride me. Please, ride me."

As if he had to ask. I was building up to it. Every time I raised my hips and lowered myself down on him, his cock hit my prostate.

There was no description I could find in all my romance books for the sounds coming out of me.

I was desperate to come, afraid that it would end and I wouldn't get more, and amazed that sex could be this good. And then I looked into Slade's eyes. That blue, like the sky on a summer day.

His hair was all tousled from where I'd pulled it, his lips were red and swollen from my kisses.

My sexy silver-fox biker was hanging by a thread.

"I'm so close, Slade."

"Me too, baby. Let go. I'll be here to catch you."

So I did. My thighs burned from exertion, sweat ran down my back. My ass burned and my cock was ready to burst.

I leaned against Slade's chest and wrapped my arms around him, feeling the cool leather jacket under my hands. In that position he was able to fuck into me at the same time as I rode him.

With my cock trapped between us, it didn't take long until the friction set off my orgasm and I spilled all over his chest.

"Aiden." He screamed into my neck as he came.

I wanted to say something, anything to tell him how good it felt, but how could I explain that?

"Best sex of my life. You may have ruined me for other men. When can we do it again?"

"Likewise. Ditto. Anytime you want."

I sat up, wincing when I realized his dick was still inside me. I lifted a little to let him slide out.

"Did I...um..."

"Say that aloud? Yes, you did."

I hid my heating face with my hand.

"Well, I guess now we know," I groaned.

"We certainly do."

SLADE

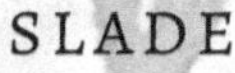

"Morning, boss...whoa...do we need an emergency coffee run?" Liam said from under the hood of a truck.

I grunted. Okay, so I was a little late coming down to the shop this morning, so what?

"Seriously, Slade. You might want to look in the mirror."

"Why?"

"Just do it."

I groaned when I realized I was wearing my shirt inside out. "I was rushing this morning," I said as a way of explanation.

"Of course you were."

I ignored his comment and pulled the shirt over my head to turn it the right way.

"Damn, Slade. I didn't know you were hiding that under your shirt."

I sighed. Just what I needed right now. Wren Mason before coffee. Or should I be relieved I hadn't been caught semi-naked by Tom instead?

"How can I help you, Wren? I haven't made up my mind about the team. To be honest, I don't think I have the time."

He crossed his arms over his chest and smiled. Wren was wearing running shorts, so the scar on his knee that had ended his pro football career was visible.

"How's your knee? I injured my shoulder years ago, and even though I'm fully recovered, it still gives me trouble when the weather changes," I said.

I walked over to the office, where I had a tray with the day's jobs, to look for the right one.

Wren walked over and leaned against the desk.

"I went running with Aiden this morning," he said, ignoring my question.

"That's nice. I didn't know he was a runner too," I replied as casually as I could, even though I was leafing through the jobs without reading any of the information on the forms.

"Yeah. He seemed a little tired today."

When I didn't say anything, Wren continued.

"Maybe you've been working him too hard."

"He's an adult, he'll know when it's too hard."

Wren snorted.

"How's his research going?"

"Don't know. Well, I think. He's a fast learner."

For the love of god, I couldn't do this without coffee. Why did everything out of my mouth sound like an innuendo?

"There's something you should know about Aiden. He doesn't always know when to stop."

What did he mean? Stop what?

I wanted to ask the question, but that would raise more questions from Wren, and I wasn't sure his visit had purely good intentions.

"Thanks for letting me know. I'll make sure to go easy on him."

"Yeah, you do...that."

He patted my shoulder and left.

"Liam, I'm going to Beans. Do you want anything?"

"No, thanks, boss. Maggie's off work today, so we're having lunch on the square."

Since Liam and Maggie had gotten together, he was different. We weren't big talkers. I always thought that was why he had fit in here with me so well from the start, but he'd definitely opened up more recently. He was more relaxed, happy, and the times when I found him staring at a tool lost in thought were fewer and far between.

He'd lost his wife not long after they were married. He hadn't known until after she'd passed, that she was pregnant with their first child. I didn't need to know the circumstances around their passing to understand the severity of the loss.

So seeing Liam find someone to love again made me wonder about things I thought couldn't happen.

I wasn't going to pretend that being with Aiden yesterday was the start of a new happy-ever-after for me. Far from it. But I also couldn't deny how great it had been to ride with someone. Share my secret spot. Talk about bikes and riding. And the sex...

Fuck, the sex had been wonderful. Even that word fell short of describing how it had been.

Spilled Beans was unusually quiet for a Monday morning, with only a few customers sitting inside, no queue, and Indy was humming to himself while writing on a blackboard behind the counter.

"Hey, Indy."

"Oh, hey, Slade. How's it going?"

"Great, thanks. Where are your customers?"

Indy chuckled and leaned on the counter to whisper. "Jake had an appointment, and my part timer is at school, so I'm on my own. I put a sign out front saying we'll have fresh cinnamon buns at eleven. It's been a blissful morning."

I didn't doubt it. Indy's pastries were to die for, so I wouldn't be surprised to see a line forming just before eleven.

"In that case, I'll have my usual coffee and two lemon muffins, please."

"Coming right up."

The bell above the coffee shop door dinged with a new customer. My smile dropped when I saw Ben grinning at me.

"Morning, Indy. Morning, Slade," he said, extra chirpy.

I smiled and nodded.

"Oh, *two* lemon muffins. I see...you're sharing those with someone?" Ben said in that casual tone that no one ever believes is casual. And of course, Indy raised his head from behind the display cabinet.

I was going to kill Tristan.

"I hear there might be an outing on Friday," I said.

"How do you know?" Indy asked with interest.

"A tall, nosy bird told me yesterday," I said, looking at Ben, who snorted.

Indy was clearly confused but confirmed their group of friends was going out to The Falls. "Are you joining us?"

"Yes, he is," Ben answered.

I took my coffee and muffins from Indy and put my money on the counter.

"Who knew I'd be back in high school at my age?" I asked and waved them goodbye.

Ben laughed.

"What was that about?" Indy asked, but I didn't hear his reply because I was already out the door.

The rest of the day was busy with customers picking up their cars and a couple of new bookings. I even spent an hour going through options for a customer who was interested in buying a Harley.

By the time Aiden walked in later in the afternoon, I was buzzing with energy and happy to have completed a chunk of tasks on my list.

"Hey," I said as he approached the checkout desk and came around the side where I sat on a barstool.

"Hey."

"Come here." I stretched out my hand until he was within reach, then I pulled him closer until he was between my legs, and kissed him.

Aiden tasted of coffee and smelled of pine, and if we weren't in my shop and risking being interrupted, I'd have already pulled his shirt up to touch his skin.

He was breathless by the time I released him.

"I...um...wasn't sure how...um, if we were going to do this again," he said.

"You mean, me staying at your place all night and sneaking out early this morning before being late for work wasn't enough to show you how much we're doing this again?"

He chuckled. "That was very college-like."

"I don't know, I didn't go to college. But it was definitely not very Slade-like."

"So we're...what are we doing? Sorry to sound like a lovesick teenager; it's not that at all."

I ran my hands over his hair. It looked too long for it to be his regular style, but I liked it. He closed his eyes when I pulled on it a little and sighed when I massaged his scalp.

"I know, Aid. Wren was here this morning."

He opened his eyes wide and tensed.

"You know they're gonna be on us like a pack of hungry wolves, right?"

"Oh god." He leaned his head against my chest. We already had a significant height difference, but this position with him between my legs, seeking comfort, made me feel things I hadn't felt in a long time.

"Aid, I know they have good intentions, but ultimately this is our business. We can tell them to back off. You know that, right?"

"Yeah, I know."

"We're two adults who happen to be ridiculously attracted to each other. I'd question your taste in men, but it's working for me, so I'll keep quiet." He slapped my chest, but I grabbed his hand and kissed it. "We're enjoying ourselves. That's it, right?"

"Right," he agreed. Something passed over his eyes, but it was gone too soon for me to see what it was. "I definitely enjoyed myself yesterday...multiple times."

I snorted.

My dick hardened at the thought of him riding me yesterday, and then how he'd taken us to the shower and sucked me until my dick came back to life before demanding I fuck him again.

My growing problem didn't go unnoticed by Aiden, who pressed closer against me and looked me in the eye, as if daring me to do something about it.

"Oh, Aiden, you're gonna be the death of me."

"But what a great way to go, right?"

I kissed his sassy mouth until he was all soft and pliant in my arms, which still didn't help my hard-on at all.

"Shop's still open, but we don't have any work to do on the bike, so what do you want to learn today?" I asked.

"Will you tell me what it's like to be in a motorcycle club?"

Hard-on sufficiently not hard anymore.

AIDEN

Slade tensed up, but then he gave me a kiss and led me to the couch in the middle of the shop.

He rarely had any customers later in the afternoon after Liam went home, but I suspected that he just enjoyed being here, catching up with paperwork with few interruptions.

"Okay, what do you want to know?" he asked.

I shrugged. "I want to know so much that I don't even know where to start. How did you get into your club? How old were you?"

"Joining an MC, that's a motorcycle club, isn't easy. You need money and connections. Remember I mentioned my neighbor that taught me how to ride?"

"Yeah."

"I basically hung around his place any time I wasn't at school since I was fourteen. He taught me everything I needed to know about bikes and helped me find a part time job at a garage. My foster parents were so happy that I was able to help them out a little that they didn't ask any questions."

Slade was staring ahead at the bikes on display in front of us while I watched him tell his story. What he was saying sounded so wholesome and good. The story of the foster kid who learned a trade and helped out his foster parents, who were actually good people. But the way he spoke, the pain in his voice was clear.

I had a strong feeling that a lot of the small decisions Slade had made because of his passion for bikes had led him down a path he later regretted. Maybe he wouldn't tell me everything, but I had to remember that he was here with me now, and he was safe.

"When I turned sixteen, I was so excited that I could finally get my license. When I got home from school, I went over to his place and just walked in, as I always did. There were a few guys there all wearing leather jackets with patches. I'd never been so impressed in my life. Even though I had no clue who they were, I wanted to be like them. Eventually my neighbor told me about the motorcycle club. He was their Road Captain. I can give you a breakdown of the ranks, but it means he had an important role, and as such, people usually listened to him. "

"So you tried to join?"

"Yeah, but I was too young. You have to be an adult to join, and you also need money and connections. I had the connections part down because of my neighbor, but I didn't have the money."

Slade went on to explain how he worked over the next two years to save as much money as he could so he could join the club.

"Before you're a fully-fledged member of an MC, there are three stages you have to pass: hang around, prospect, and probation."

"Let me guess, you were already hanging around, so you went straight to the second stage," I joked.

Slade laughed. "Yeah, you're right. The clubhouse was outside of town, but for some reason they liked hanging around my neighborhood. When I turned eighteen, I already had enough money saved to join. I was sponsored by my neighbor and became a prospect."

I didn't miss that with all the information he'd shared so far, Slade hadn't actually said where he came from or the name of his neighbor. My curiosity spiked, but he was giving me the information that would help my story. The details were irrelevant.

"I guess after you became a prospect, everything changed for you."

"Yeah."

Slade went quiet, so I accepted that was as much as I'd get from him.

"Is this hard for you to talk about?" I asked.

"Not as much as I thought. It's mostly bringing back memories... I haven't talked about this in a very long time."

"I understand."

He smiled. "You know how tough everyone thinks bikers are?"

I nodded.

"The president was a neat freak. I mean, all bikers are a bit like that, but mostly with their bikes. This guy wanted everything around him in its place. So, more often than not, I found myself cleaning up after the guys and cleaning the club-house. I took such pride in it."

"Do you think that gave you something you didn't get at home?"

Slade looked at me with the same expression he had that first night at Benny's Diner.

"Yes. I didn't know it at the time. I thought I was being a rebel. When I finished high school, I started working full-time at the garage. I'd aged out of the system, so I should have been kicked out of my foster parents' home, but my mom got sick and they couldn't foster anymore. I stayed with them another year to help out around the house before I left."

"Why did you leave?"

"To keep them safe."

I reached out to run my hand through his hair, feeling nothing but relief when Slade leant into my hand. "Maybe we should—"

My words were interrupted by someone walking in the shop.

"Hey, Slade, I think I'm ready," the guy said.

Slade turned to me. "We had a part delivery. It's on the workbench if you want to check it out, this shouldn't take long."

"Okay."

The big metal door to the garage was shut, so I was surprised when I got to the garage and saw a bundle of ginger fur on top of the delivery box.

"Hey, buddy, it's you again."

The kitten raised its head and stared at me with big green eyes. I couldn't tell why, but I had a feeling she was a girl.

"Do you live here?" I asked and got a little meow as an answer.

I raised my hand slowly to see what kind of reaction I got and was surprised to see her bumping her head against my hand. She wasn't as flighty or aggressive as she'd been the other day.

"What's your name, beautiful?"

She meowed again.

"I don't speak cat, so you're going to have to help me out here, okay?"

Another bump to my hand.

"I'm not going to invade your privacy, so meow if you're a boy and purr if you're a girl."

I chuckled to myself. I must be losing my mind, but I glanced behind me to the shop and Slade was deep in conversation with the guy, checking something on his computer.

The kitten stood up on the box and did a turn before sitting on its back legs, purring.

"Okay, you're a girl. Thank you for letting me know. Now your name... Ginger?"

She hissed. "Okay, okay, point taken."

"So you're not..." She hissed again. "The name I'm not going to repeat. Sorry if it's a sensitive topic. I know how you feel, I used to get called magnolia at school because I'm so pasty white." I shrugged.

"Hmm, okay, so you clearly live here, even though Slade never mentioned owning a cat. Do you want to give me a clue?"

She meowed again and then jumped from the box onto the workbench and then the floor. She walked around the frame of the Harley, getting a little too close.

"What are you trying to tell me?"

She jumped onto the bike frame. I gasped and closed my eyes, praying to the god of bikes, if there was one, for the frame of the Harley to stay upright on the stand.

"Oh my god, the Harley."

The cat meowed, so I opened my eyes again to see her perfectly balanced on the frame.

"Harley."

She meowed again.

"Is that your name? Harley?"

It totally made sense now. Only Slade would have a cat and name it after his favorite bike.

"Well, hello, Harley. Nice to meet you," I said.

Harley jumped from the bike frame straight onto the workbench, making my heart skip another three beats.

She sat on the box again. "I guess you're not helping me with this delivery, are you?"

Harley purred and raised her paw as if she wanted to play.

"I think you better scoot before your daddy comes over and tells us both off."

She jumped back on the floor and left the garage through the gap under the metal door.

Slade was still with his customer, so I allowed myself a moment to admire him from afar.

I wondered if he ever noticed how often he stroked his beard. The man was sex on legs and, okay, I'd always had a thing for older men, but Slade was more than his appearance.

The way he'd cared for me yesterday had been unexpected.

With Richard, I'd felt like I was always playing the same part. Even though we were both versatile, it had been rare when he'd let me top him. And if he was extra horny, he could be rough to the point of pain.

I pushed those thoughts aside in favor of memories from yesterday. We hadn't switched, but there was something about Slade that told me we could have. I'd been so desperate to have him that I hadn't given him a chance. He'd only drawn the line at taking me twice so I wouldn't end up too sore.

"I thought I was the only one who got hard staring at bikes."

I snapped up to see Slade leaning against the door separating the shop from the garage, a heated smile on his face.

"Harley kept me company while you were busy, but I was actually just thinking about you," I said, walking over to him until we were only inches apart.

"Oh really? And what were you thinking about that caused that problem in your jeans?"

"Unless you suffer from short-term memory loss, you'll know exactly what I was thinking," I said in my best attempt to sound seductive.

He put his hands on either side of my face and pulled me in for a kiss that ignited the need for Slade that hadn't really gone away since he'd left my apartment very early this morning.

"Hmm...I remember now. You see, us old folks sometimes have a hard time remembering things."

I wanted to make a joke about how hard he was, but he

kissed me again, and then I was the one with the memory loss problem.

"How about I take you to dinner? I just sold a new bike, so we can celebrate...and if you're lucky, you can have me for desser—"

"Deal."

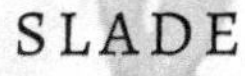

I closed the shop and grabbed the paperwork to lock it in my office.

Aiden had been meticulously buffing the engine case for the Harley, following my instructions, while I'd dealt with another bike purchase inquiry.

Business was good, and I'd been spending all my free time with Aiden. Not all of it with clothes on.

In fact, while initially Aiden had been as shy about being with me as he was upfront about what he wanted, in the last week, he'd let go of all his hang-ups, whatever they might be.

We'd even switched from having dinner at Benny's every night to eating in, or ordering in when we couldn't be bothered to cook. Or to be more exact, when we'd been so tired from having sex that we couldn't be bothered to cook.

"Are you going to stand there and ogle me all day?"

Would the answer to that question ever be no, especially when Aiden had such a perfect ogle-worthy ass?

"Aid, you're bending over my workbench, operating a handheld drill. You have no idea how much self-restraint I need right now to keep my clothes on."

He stopped the drill, which he was using to buff the

engine casing of the Harley, and removed his protective face mask.

"Well, don't mind me. All the doors are closed. It's just you, me...and the power drill."

I groaned when he shifted his weight from one foot to the other. His ass was basically saying "come get me."

Fucking tease.

I walked over to him, sparing a glance at the clock on the wall that told me we still had time before we needed to leave to meet the guys at the bar.

"Were you doing that on purpose?" I asked, running my hand over his ass. He bent over a little more to press against my front. The bastard.

"Doing what on purpose?" he said with the least innocent expression I'd ever seen on him.

"Do you know what happens to sassy boys who think they're in charge?"

He trapped his lower lip between his teeth. "No?"

"You're not tricking anyone, baby. So you're going to bend over while I eat your sweet ass. No coming until I say so. Got it?"

He looked at me from under his lashes.

"Yes...boss."

"Don't call me boss. Liam calls me boss. It's just weird."

"Okay...Daddy."

"Please don't," I chuckled.

"Okay, then, what can I call you?"

There was an air of defiance in his eyes. I pulled him so he was straight up against my chest and claimed his mouth without turning him around. It was a difficult position for a kiss because he was twisting his neck, but he didn't seem to mind since he gave as good as he got.

"Yours," I moaned into his mouth. "Call me yours."

"Mine, definitely mine."

I ended the kiss before I came in my pants like a teenager.

That's how Aiden made me feel, except there was no denying that I definitely wasn't a young man anymore.

My recovery time was long, which actually suited me fine because I could give Aiden extra orgasms, but my back was giving me trouble.

Aiden had noticed it when I'd had a crippling spasm during sex a few days ago and we'd had to stop. Coming prematurely would have been less embarrassing.

Speaking of which, maybe I shouldn't get on my knees on a hard floor as much as I had a hard-on for eating Aiden's ass.

"Change of plans," I said, pulling Aiden toward the staff area.

"What? No fair," he complained, but still removed his clothes extra fast when he saw we were headed for the shower.

I was definitely thankful to past-Slade for having a wet room with a bench and hooks rather than just a cubicle shower.

Aiden turned the water on and pulled us straight under the shower.

"Fuck, that's cold. Are you actively trying to not get laid right now?" I asked, looking down at my cock with pity.

Aiden got on his knees, taking my cock in the wet heat of his mouth as far as he could manage.

The water warmed up at the same time as fire built inside me.

"Fuck, you have an amazing mouth, baby," I moaned.

"I know," he said, letting go of me with a pop and crawling over to where his jeans were to grab a condom and lube.

His shirt fell off the hook and onto the wet floor, but Aiden was a man on a mission to get me inside him. No need for the five-second, self-destroying warning.

Thirty minutes later, we were on our way to The Falls, a bar on the outskirts of Chester Falls.

The Falls had a good atmosphere. With the dark woods, live music, and friendly staff, it was a great place to come for a drink or two. It didn't hurt that it had a wonderful view of the waterfalls that gave the town its name.

In this summer weather, their deck was perfect to chill with friends. Even if those friends were almost half my age. I ignored my internal self-jab and told Aiden to find the guys while I got us drinks.

"Hey, Daddy, what can I get you?" Brent, the bartender, said.

He was a really friendly guy and, so far, I hadn't seen anyone he didn't flirt with. I wasn't sure if that was just who he was as a person or a requirement of the job. He only ever took it as far as he needed to get a smile out of his customer, so I assumed it was the latter option.

"Do I really give out the Daddy-vibe?"

He was preparing a cocktail but stopped and leaned over the counter a little.

"Let me see...you're tall, hot, a total silver-fox, those eyes could stop butter from melting at your request. So yeah...if it's your thing, then..." he shrugged.

I shook my head. "Not my thing. Wren's group is outside, do they all have drinks?"

"They got a round a while ago, and could probably do with another one."

"Can you sort me out?"

"Sure, Daddy."

I laughed at his sugary sweet but teasing voice. The kid was a good bartender.

Balancing all the drinks on a tray was not easy. That was a strikeout for jobs I could do for fun in my retirement.

"I rode Slade's bike," Aiden said proudly as I placed the tray on the table.

"I bet you did, you bad boy," Tom replied.

"I've never seen anyone riding Slade's bike, so you must be special." Wren said. "Can you get him to join the adult football team too?"

"No." Aiden said so quickly everyone's eyes were on him.

He blushed a very pretty pink, that I now knew went all over when he was worked up.

"What Aiden means is that I hurt my back this week, so I probably shouldn't play any kind of contact sports."

Aiden's face turned to me so fast that I wondered if he'd hurt his neck. "Like, *no* contact sports?"

I heard a snort from the other side of the table. Aiden was *not* as quiet as he thought he was.

"Well, maybe a few select contact sports," I whispered in his ear, kissing the lobe before I pulled back.

Wren stood up and stretched out his hand, wiggling his fingers. "Come on guys, pay up."

"Oh, come on, that's not fair. I had less information to go by," Indy said.

Tate took out a bill from his wallet and gave it to Wren, promising Indy he'd let him win later.

Tristan and Ben followed, with Tristan muttering he should have known better and not trusted horny old men...or something of the kind.

"Can I pay you in blow—" Wren covered up Tom's mouth with his hand and said, "Yes, you can."

"What's going on?" Aiden asked.

Everyone looked around, avoiding eye contact.

"What's going on, if I can take a guess, is that your friends placed a bet on us," I said, finally giving up the pretense and placing my arm over Aiden's chair and around his shoulders.

Tom gave a loud sigh and moved to sit on Wren's lap. "Isn't love wonderful, babe?"

"Wait a minute," Aiden said. "How did you all know? Except for my runs in the morning with Wren, I haven't even seen you."

There was a collective snort, including from me, which got me the side-eye from Aiden.

"Oh, my darling second best friend Aiden," Wren said.

Tom was looking at him like a kitten ready to be stroked to sleep.

"First of all, you've really slowed down on our runs, like waaaaay down," he said.

"So what? I've been tired, and it's a forest, *not* the paved ground of the beach walk in San Diego."

"Plus, Benny said you were there every night last week for dinner, but not this week."

"Traitor," Aiden muttered between his teeth.

"And you're literally wearing Slade's shirt."

Aiden stared down at the shirt with the logo of my shop that I'd given him to wear after his had gotten wet earlier, and then looked at me.

I shrugged and pulled him in for a kiss.

He melted into my touch immediately. I knew he'd be beet red by the time we were done with the kiss, but I also wanted him to relax and stop worrying.

From the loud cheers around us, I took it that his friends approved.

Fuck my life. Fuck alcohol and fuck hangovers.

"I hate Wren," I moaned into my pillow.

"That's not what you were saying last night. I would have been jealous if you hadn't gone on a ten-minute speech about how platonic your love is, how Tom should definitely not feel threatened, how you'd totally join them for a threesome, and if I'm not mistaken, you offered me to the whole group, saying everyone should ride my bike. *That* was not a euphemism. Or at least it's not when you stare at my crotch as you say it."

I groaned, which made my head hurt.

"Why are you here? Let me die of mortification or dehydration or something."

"Come here, sweetheart."

I kept my eyes closed because it hurt too much to open them but scooted closer to Slade.

He ran his magical fingers over my head, massaging my temples and then my scalp. "My poor baby."

"Hmmm."

I rarely drank, which was why I felt like death would have been a less harsh sentence to last night's outing. And the worst was that I didn't even suffer from alcohol-induced amnesia. Nope. I remembered every single stupid thing that came out of my mouth.

Oh fuck.

"Slade?"

"Yes, sweetie?"

My belly filled up with butterflies at the term of endearment.

"I have questions."

"Okay?"

"How did I get home last night?"

"You were too drunk to be safe on the bike, even with me riding, so I put you in a cab and followed the cab home. We're at my place, by the way."

"We are?" I tried to open my eyes, but nope, it was too early.

"Yeah, I thought you might be unwell today, and I also needed clean pants. As it turns out, my laundry doesn't do itself when I'm not here." His chuckle made everything move, but it felt nice. Everything he did felt nice.

"Another question. Um...did I really talk about my ex?"

"Richard the Tiny Dick? Yup. At length. It was quite amusing. I mean, I'd totally throat-punch the guy if I saw him, but I'm happy to know my dick is better than his...*even* if everyone in the bar now also knows."

Jesus fucking Christ, I was never ever in my whole life, however long it may be, going to have another drink. Ever.

"I'm sorry," I said into his chest.

A phone rang, louder than it should in my opinion. It wasn't my ringtone, so I covered up my head with the bedsheet.

When it stopped, Slade turned back to me. I know this because he kissed my forehead like a gentleman. I knew he was hard. He normally was in the morning—so much for complaining about his age—but he wasn't pushing me for sex.

I hated that the thought that Richard would have behaved differently was even crossing my mind. He had no place anywhere I happened to be, and certainly not when I was with Slade.

"Open your eyes, baby," he said softly.

I did, and this time it didn't feel so bad.

"Hi," I said.

"Good morning, gorgeous. Do you want coffee?"

I nodded.

"Okay, you stay here, don't do anything wild, and I'll come back in a minute with some coffee, toast, and a painkiller, okay?"

God, I love this man.

I opened my eyes so wide that I felt like I was being stabbed all the way to my brain. What the fuck? What kind of weird thought was that?

Temporary. This was temporary because I'd nearly met all of my objectives when I left San Diego, and I'd be ready to go back shortly.

I even took my fingers out to count them.

One. Take a break to cleanse from Richard because, even after almost a year, his presence somehow still permeated the walls of my apartment.

Two. See Wren and the guys.

Three. Research for my secret release. The one that no one knew about so it didn't create a frenzy of questions, because as far as everyone knew, A. Lawton was on a break.

Four. Four...what the fuck was four? Ah well, those were enough. I'd done those, right? Maybe another week or two and then I'd be back home, and Slade would be just a nice memory. A reminder that I wasn't the broken man Richard had left behind.

God, I hated getting drunk. I was always so fucking emotional.

I looked around to familiarize myself with Slade's place. I

wasn't sure what to expect, but the best description I had for Slade's room was a sanctuary. The bed was huge and it was pillow central. I never knew you could fit so many pillows on a bed and still sleep comfortably.

The walls were painted a light grey and there were large photos on the walls. Landscapes, roads, buildings. I wondered what significance, if any, they had to Slade.

"Oh, you're up."

I sat back against the headboard, fluffing at least three pillows.

"There's a ninety-five percent chance I'll never leave this bed again. Just saying."

He smiled, putting two painkillers in my hand and holding the cup of coffee. "What does the missing five percent account for?"

"I'm gonna need to pee soon."

"You're something else, Aid—"

The phone rang again. Slade looked at it as if he wanted to throw it out of the window.

"What's up? Who is it?" I asked.

He silenced the phone and put it back on the bedside table.

"My ex-husband."

Slade had an ex-husband? He'd left a lot of personal stuff out of his conversations, but somehow I had assumed he'd always been single.

"Should you...um, talk to him?" I asked. We weren't in a relationship, were we? We were only two people who enjoyed each other. Surely he should find out what his ex wanted.

"I don't have anything to say to him. Aiden, we divorced six years ago, and I haven't seen or spoken to him since. There's absolutely no reason for us to talk again."

Maybe he was saying it to reassure me, or to reassure himself, but he didn't seem convinced.

"I think you should take the call next time. If he already called a few times today, and from your face it's not just today, then something must be up."

Slade caressed my cheek and leaned over for a kiss. "I'll call him tomorrow. Today is our underwear day."

"Underwear day?"

"Underwear day."

True to his word, we spent the whole day in just our underwear. I had a chance to inspect his book collection, which he was only a little embarrassed about when I pointed out most of his books were mine, and he even had some titles twice that I'd recovered for a new edition.

We cooked together, laughed, and made out...a lot.

"You are a fun guy, Slade," I said when we sat on his couch after dinner. It was still early, so the sun wasn't completely gone yet. In fact, his couch was in the perfect spot to relax with the setting sun shining on us.

Slade had my feet on his lap and was massaging them gently. I was doing the same to him.

"I can't say I've ever been told that I'm a fun guy," he chuckled. "Moody? Quiet? Yes. Fun? Nope."

"Well, maybe people weren't paying attention."

"Can I ask you a question?"

"Sure."

"Why haven't you published in a year?"

I knew he'd ask the question at some point, but it was still hard to talk about it.

"How much do you know about me?" I asked.

"Only what you've told me. I've never looked you up, and I'm not on social media nor do I read gossip news."

"You might be the only person out there that has the chance to hear the version of events from me. It's a first.'

Slade held out his hand, so I reached out with mine, and he turned me over so I sat between his legs and against his chest. I leaned my head back, taking comfort from his warmth and the smell of his shower soap.

"I met Richard at an author conference a few years ago. He's an agent, so he was outgoing, talked to everyone, and hard to say no to. We were happy for a while until I started making serious money. My family comes from money and I moved to San Diego to get away from all that, but when my bank account became too much for me to manage, I asked my parents for advice. They thought I was ready to get back to the Manhattan scene, so they traveled to San Diego, and that's when they met Richard."

"Were there problems between them? I mean, your folks aren't homophobic, are they?"

"No, they don't really care about that. Richard charmed the pants off them both, especially my mother. After they left, he wouldn't stop talking about them, and even suggested we move to New York. It took me a long time to realize it was all about the money."

Slade wrapped his arms tighter around me and kissed my hair.

"What happened a year ago that made you stop publishing?"

"He became more insistent about moving near my parents and even used my mom to set me up for a secret wedding. Of course, my mom thought everything was great and we were madly in love. We weren't. I said no to the proposal, and that I needed a prenup, as it was a condition of my trust fund. Without a prenup, I would never be able to access any of my money."

The image of Richard's shocked face when I'd told him the lie was still vivid in my mind. He was so angry; to the point I was afraid he'd become aggressive.

My neighbors had called the police because of the noise. I'd never been so embarrassed in my whole life. The camel didn't need another straw to break its back, but getting a call from the guy he was fucking behind my back had definitely done it.

"Aiden, we may only be temporary, but I need you to listen to me. You're more than your money. You're the most amazing person I know, and you're beautiful, kind, and special. Do you hear me?"

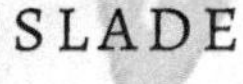

SLADE

*H*is silence broke my heart until I felt him nod against me.

"You know what was the worst? I've always been a private person. I have someone that deals with my social media accounts and they're only about my publishing. But within days of Richard leaving, loads of private information was leaked and I was tagged in all of it. Things I'd only told him about my relationship with my parents and how I wanted to make my own way in life. It was all out there, and it was so embarrassing. My parents stopped talking to me. They blamed me for the breakup. After that, I couldn't write. I was in the middle of a book and I couldn't pick it up. I sat at my desk for days, but all I could see in front of me were those lies on the internet, the stuff that was true but private."

His voice sounded so broken. Had Aiden ever told this to anyone? Wren? I was absolutely sure that if he knew, his friendly warning about Aiden would have carried a lot more weight.

If Aiden only knew how I much understood his pain. How much I still carried it.

"Come with me," I said in his ear and made a move to get

up. He followed me to the bedroom and didn't complain when I removed his boxer shorts and asked him to lay down on the bed.

His dick was soft, as was mine. This wasn't time for sex. I just needed to offer him some comfort and be close to him.

"When did you get your idea for your book?" I asked.

"I was in line to get a coffee after my morning run. There was this little girl with her mom outside the coffee shop. The girl had a pink backpack and they looked like they were waiting for someone. After a few minutes I heard the rumble of a bike and this really tough-looking guy wearing full-on leather gear stopped his bike right in front of the little girl. I've never seen someone so happy. When he took his helmet off, my heart just melted. The way he gazed at that girl was as if she was the most priceless thing. I couldn't hear what they said to each other, but it didn't matter. In my head, I was already forming my own story."

I ran my hand over his cheek, feeling the rough scruff of his unshaved beard under my thumb.

"I'm glad you found your inspiration. I've missed your stories, and I just know this one is going to be even better."

He chuckled. "Because it has a biker?"

"No, because you're free now. Because I think the Aiden in front of me at this moment, gloriously naked under my bed sheets, is a different person to the guy in the designer shirt that stole my book at the fair."

"I didn't steal—" I laughed, even as I shut him up with a kiss.

It was tender and sweet, and I had to remind myself of the words I said when we were on the couch. This was temporary.

Waking up with Aiden wrapped around me was good any day, but on a Sunday, when we had nowhere else to be, it was absolute perfection.

Light streamed from the gap between the curtains. I had no idea what time it was, but I had no wish to move out of bed, not when Aiden was still snoring lightly against my chest.

His hand rested over my heart and his fingers twitched every so often, as if he was having a dream. Behind him there was a barrier of pillows nested against his back. It was as if overnight he'd built himself a cozy fort made of me and my pillows.

I ran my hand through his tousled brown hair, glad he didn't even stir. I needed a little more time before he woke up. There were feelings bubbling inside me that I hadn't felt in a long time, and I needed to process them.

Last night I'd continued reminding myself that what Aiden and I had was temporary, but there was a strong voice in my head that kept repeating over and over again "why."

After my divorce, I'd decided I couldn't do to another man what I'd done to Mike. The secrets about my past had eaten me up inside and ultimately damaged our relationship. But the longer I spent with Aiden, the more I wondered if it would be different this time.

I'd met Mike at a crossroads in my life. In order to stay on the right path, I'd needed to keep my secrets, leave them there so I wouldn't be tempted to turn around. In twenty-five years, I'd never even looked at the line, let alone cross it.

Would I have a chance with Aiden if I opened up to him? Would he still want me afterward? I didn't even know if he wanted me now. At least not for more than our current casual arrangement.

"I can hear your thoughts from here and the answer is yes."

I looked down at Aiden, who was clearly no longer asleep, with confusion.

"Oh really? And what was I thinking about?" I asked.

He pulled my nipple into a hard peak and then moved his hand lower until he found my cock. I swallowed when he wrapped around my length and gave it a tight squeeze and a long, slow stroke.

"You were saying: Aiden, I'm dying to feel you inside me, please fuck me before I die."

I snorted. "I never knew you were a mind reader as well as a talented author."

He raised himself on his elbows. "Really?"

"Yeah, your hand is down there, please tell me you can feel how hard I am at the thought of you fucking me."

"Yeah, but...I was joking, you don't have to."

"Aid, I know, but I want to. I told you I like to switch, I just haven't done it in a while."

He climbed on top of me and took my mouth like a starved man. I liked it. No, I loved it.

God, I was so fucked.

"Shit, what's the time?" Aiden asked.

I grabbed my phone from the bedside table and pressed the home button to show him.

"Shit, I have a run with Wren, and he'll never let me live it down if I'm late. Slade, this is going to be dirty and quick," he said.

I licked a path from his neck all the way up his chin and took his mouth, all while wrapping my legs around his waist. I was older, but I still had some moves.

"Baby, make it real dirty, and you can be as quick as you like."

He threw himself over the pillows on his side of the bed to get to the other bedside table, where he already knew I had condoms and lube.

"One of these days I'm going to get oil all over this hot body of yours and I'm going to fuck you right up against that workbench you keep so neat and tidy."

Aiden's dirty talk was enough to rile me up with such need that I barely even flinched when his fingers worked to stretch me.

"More," I growled.

"Oh, you like it like that? Turn around."

Fuck, his commanding voice was going to make me come before he put his cock inside me.

I grabbed two pillows and placed them under me, tucking my hard cock between them. Aiden placed himself between my legs, running his hand up the backs of my thighs as if he had all the time in the world.

"I thought you had somewhere to be."

"It's cute you think you're in charge here," he chuckled.

I was going to retort back when I felt his cock push through the rim of my ass. I rested my head on my forearms and relaxed as much as I could.

The burn was there, unmistakable, but unlike times when I'd bottomed for Mike, my brain went somewhere else. Suddenly I was super-aware of the way Aiden's legs brushed against the back of mine. How his breaths were shallow against my back, as if he were battling with himself.

It wasn't until he was all the way inside me that I let out a full breath. He lay on my back, his head between my shoulder blades, but when he spoke it was as if he was whispering directly in my ear.

"I hope you're ready for it, Slade, because your ass is hugging my cock like a motherfucking tight glove and I'm not gonna last."

"Talk dirty to me like that and I'll be the one who—fuck."

Words left me when he withdrew almost all the way and pushed in again.

"That's it, Slade. Take it all as I drive in and out of you. You feel so tight, so hot. I'm going to fuck you so good you'll remember this every time you move until I'm back and we get to do it all over again."

"Yes, fuck, yes."

My strategic placement of my dick between the pillows and the way he was driving into me was making me fly to heights I never thought possible.

"Aid, I'm so close."

He put his arms under mine and reached for my hands, lacing them together.

"Do you need help?" he asked, but I shook my head. No hands needed, and that was a definite first.

"No, just fuck me hard, I need it."

I was surrounded by Aiden. In me, on me, he was everything. My orgasm came hard and fast. I knew the pillows would be ruined, but I'd buy a million pillows if I needed.

"Slade." Aiden shouted as his orgasm took over him, and there was an unmistakable stinging on my back that I bet had Aiden's teeth marks written all over it.

He withdrew his spent cock from my ass, collapsing on his back next to me with the biggest grin on his face.

"Show off," I teased, even as I pulled him in for a kiss.

A quick shower later and he was walking out to meet Wren, wearing a pair of my shorts and an old T-shirt of mine. Nothing ever felt so right.

My phone rang sometime later, and since I'd promised Aiden I'd hear Mike out, I answered it.

"Hello?"

"Why the fuck haven't you been answering my calls?"

I wanted to say a few choice words, but there was an edge to his voice. I'd known him for far too long to ignore that.

"What's going on, Mike?"

"I need you to come home, Uncle Ted is in the hospital... Slade, it's not good."

AIDEN

"So...you and Slade, huh?"

"Don't give yourself a stitch, breathe."

Wren slowed down and laughed.

"I've lost count of the times we've talked through a five-mile run stitch free, and now you're claiming amateur status? No way."

I smiled. When he'd texted asking if we were running, I knew he just wanted some time alone to talk. It didn't mean I was going to make it easy on him.

"I think you're just finding an excuse to cut the run short. Is Tom tiring you more than usual?"

"I could ask the same of you." He looked at his wristwatch. "You do realize in the old days we'd be on the way back, right?"

Yeah, I was aware of that, as much as I was aware of how much my thighs ached from fucking Slade this morning. I'd have asked him to stay in bed until I got back, for a repeat, but I needed to get back to the apartment to pick up my notes and my laptop.

Slade had asked me to spend the night with him again and there was as much a chance of me saying no as there was of me avoiding this conversation with Wren. But I did need my stuff, so we'd agreed I'd get back to his place in time for a late lunch.

"What do you want to know?" I asked.

"Length, width, and thrusting power."

I coughed. "What?"

"Jesus, man, your face just now," he laughed, and I hoped he got a stitch. It would serve him right. "I was joking. I can see by your blissed-out face that there are no issues in that area. Way to go, Aid."

"Um, thanks?"

He slowed his pace down to a fast walk.

"How did you guys go from him helping you out with research to...whatever it is you're doing? I mean, I knew you had a thing for older guys, but since you've been with The Tiny Dick for so long..."

I snorted. Wren had been calling Richard "The Tiny Dick" since I had told him about one of our first arguments. It stuck, but it was just between us. I guessed Richard had been downgraded now.

Wren slowed his pace to a stroll, which meant things were about to get serious.

"I'm going straight to the point, Aid. What's going to happen to you when you go back home?"

"We agreed this is casual while I'm here. That's all. There's no point denying ourselves when we know we're attracted to each other. It's been a while since Richard, so I think I've earned some fun, haven't I?" There was a slight bite to my voice, and I didn't know if it was as a response to Wren's question, or if what I'd said sounded a lot like bullshit to me.

"That's not what I meant, Aid. What's going to happen to *you* when it's over."

"Why?"

He sighed. "Aid, I've known you a long time, but I've only known you after Tiny Dick. The Aiden I saw two days ago was a different person. You were carefree, happy, and I dare to say, in love."

"Don't be silly." I laughed, but it sounded wrong even to me.

Wren stopped completely and put his hands on my shoulders. "Look at you. You're wearing his clothes for goodness sake. Have you even been home since Friday?"

I shook my head.

"I can see you have feelings for him and, based on his behavior on Friday, he feels the same way."

"I don't know," I confessed. Did I want to believe Wren? Hell yeah. But as much as my confidence had grown since being with Slade, I was still afraid to take such a big risk.

Breaking up with Richard took a toll on me, not because of us, but because of what he did.

If Slade didn't return my feelings and didn't want a relationship with me...I didn't think I'd survive that. Which told me exactly how deep my feelings for him went.

"Hey, come here." Wren hugged me tight. "I wish I could take back all the things Tiny Dick did to you, but since I can't, I'm going to say this, and I hope you're listening to me. You have a family here. Slade or no Slade, if San Diego becomes too lonely you will be welcomed here."

"Thank you. I know that...I do...and I'll think about it."

"Okay, how about we race back? Tom is making brownies, so I need to burn some calories before I spend the rest of the day eating chocolate off him."

"TMI, Wren. TMI."

"Like you don't want to do the same," he snorted before he took off running.

I had a second shower at the apartment, grabbed my stuff and walked back to Slade's place.

Since I'd been in Chester Falls, my car had been thoroughly neglected, and I couldn't bring myself to regret it. It felt good to walk into town along the river path, and whenever

Slade and I worked late, he'd sometimes take me home on his bike.

I was avoiding thinking of my return to San Diego, as much as it was also constantly in the back of my mind. There was no question that I needed to get back, but the thought of stepping into my much larger apartment didn't hold any appeal. To think I'd once thought it was the perfect place for me. View of the ocean, lots of light from the floor-to-ceiling windows, it was perfect for someone who worked from home. But was it still?

When Slade opened the door to his place, I knew something wasn't right. I put my bag on the floor by the door and took the box with the apple pies that I'd picked up from Benny's into the kitchen.

Slade sat on his couch facing the window, wearing an expression I couldn't decipher.

I was relieved when I made a gesture for him to scoot over and he did, so I wedged myself between him and the arm of the couch. He didn't complain when I put my arms around him, in fact, as soon as I did, he leaned back and laced our fingers together.

"What happened?"

"Mike called again. His uncle is in the hospital."

"I'm so sorry to hear that, sweetheart. Are you close to him?"

Slade's voice was low and laced with pain. "He saved my life."

I wanted to know the story behind that statement, but it was only another piece of the puzzle that was Slade Warren. Maybe one day I'd see the whole thing complete, or maybe not, but this wasn't about me.

"How serious is it? Should you go see him?"

"I don't know. How serious it is, I mean. Mike just told me to come home."

"Do you think he would say that lightly?"

"No. Mike loves his uncle like a father. Ted...he's...fuck, I don't know what to do. I haven't seen him or talked to him since I left Atlanta. He's an amazing man. He gave me a job at his garage when I had nothing but my bike and the clothes I was wearing."

I kissed the side of his head, and he let out a sigh. "I've never looked back, Aid. Always kept moving. I'm scared that once I go back for one thing, it'll force me to face the rest."

"Revisiting the past isn't always bad. We change as we grow. Sometimes going back means you can bury the past and put it to rest. Which...fuck...that's not what I meant about your uncle. Shit."

How un-fucking-sensitive was I? In trying to make things better for Slade, I was basically saying he was going to Atlanta for a funeral.

Slade chuckled. "You are such a writer, baby. Don't worry. I know what you meant. Maybe you're right. I love Ted. He was part of my life for such a long time, and if he's not well then I need to put my shit to one side and go see him."

"Do you want me to come with you?"

Slade turned around in my arms and I braced myself for the rejection.

"I couldn't ask that of you, Aid. You have your own work to do."

I remembered my conversation with Wren and decided to push it.

"Slade, I care about you. Let me go with you for support. It's what, an eight, nine-hour drive? When we get there, I can be with you as much or as little as you want. We can book a hotel room and I can stay away if you'd rather be with your family."

"I'd really like that. Thank you."

Slade's kisses always took my breath away, but this one felt even more reverent than usual. As though he didn't know how to thank me with words. If only he knew there was nothing to thank me for. I'd be there for him any time.

"Right, now that we have that sorted, who wants a slice of apple pie?" I said, pulling on his beard.

"God you're an amazing man, Aiden Lawton."

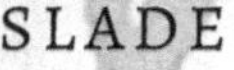

"Who's going to keep an eye on Harley?" Aiden asked.

Weird question, but it was early in the day. "Liam will make sure nothing happens to her."

"Okay, that's good. Right, I'm driving, which means you're the deejay. A word of warning. I take my driving music very seriously," Aiden said, giving me a side-look and a smile before focusing back to the road.

The sun was barely up in the sky. Aiden had suggested we travel earlier in the morning rather than set off immediately and need an extra night halfway to Atlanta.

I felt a lot more rested this morning than I thought I would. I had Aiden to thank for that, too, because he'd taken care of me in every sense of the word.

We'd had Momma Ruth's apple pie from Benny's, and then I'd packed my stuff and taken Aiden back to his place so he could grab more clothes. When we got back, he cooked us dinner, keeping me distracted throughout by doing it buck naked.

After dinner he decided we should pick random books from my bookshelf and read the sex scenes aloud. It didn't take long until we broke down in fits of laughter at how silly they all sounded when read out of context.

Laughter gave way to making out, which gave way to making love.

I took the opportunity that Aiden was driving to check him out. He'd given me so much last night. There was no mistake there, we'd made love to each other.

The heat was there, as was his dirty talk. Who knew he had such a dirty mouth when he topped? I'd happily bottom for the rest of my life just to hear him give himself over to the power of his body and the need to chase his orgasm.

"I can feel your eyes on me. And no, no blowjobs while I'm driving."

I laughed aloud.

"What, are you saying I was the only one thinking that? Damn," he said.

I connected my phone to his car and looked for the music streaming app.

"Before you do that, can I ask you a question?"

"Sure." I put the phone on my lap and turned in my seat to face him.

"I've been working through my plot and trying to figure out my character's connection to the motorcycle club, what he did there, but also how he got out. Although I'm not sure I want him out. I don't want him to give up something that is so important to him."

"What kind of business does the MC do?"

"What do you mean?"

"Remember I told you how the MC is like a family business. You have a hierarchy, which dictates what kind of power each member has. MCs also run businesses, and they vary from doing charitable work to illegal stuff and everything in between."

Aiden seemed to think about it for a moment. "I'd like them to do charitable things. The conflict between my characters is the reason they separated, heightened by the time they spent apart. The other guy made assumptions about what kind of stuff bikers do, so I'd like my biker to show the reader that he's not a bad guy."

I liked Aiden's idea. Selfishly, I hadn't wanted his character to be an outlaw.

"And who's your other guy?"

"He's an elementary school teacher. They bump into each other because the husband of the school's principal is in the same MC as my biker. There's an event at school and my biker goes in to give a talk about safety on the road."

"Let me guess, the teacher has all these assumptions about bikers, and at the end of the speech he goes over to his old friend and goes on a rant about how dare he come to his school?"

Aiden laughed. "Yeah, like that."

"Ooh, is there going to be hate sex?" I asked and then lowered my voice. "I love how you write your sex scenes."

I didn't miss Aiden's cock hardening. If there wasn't a chance we'd end up dead on the side of the road, I'd be whipping it out and sucking it like a lollipop.

"Whatever you're thinking about, don't," he warned. "Let's listen to some music before I stop the car and make you blow me."

I debated the merits of that, but decided he was right and looked up a Bon Jovi playlist.

"Good choice. The ultimate silver-fox," he said.

"Hey! You know he's ten years older than me, right?"

He raised one hand off the steering wheel and counted on his fingers. "One, I told you I don't care about age. Two, if he was inclined toward men I'd totally do him. Three, don't worry, I'd still have enough energy to do you after. Or maybe at the same time."

I ran my hands over my face and groaned. He was going to be the death of me.

We caught some heavy traffic on the way into Atlanta, so we went straight to the hotel and ordered room service.

The long drive made us both tired, so after dinner we settled in bed, facing each other and talking about everything and nothing.

Now I knew Aiden hated Ramen as much as he hated designer clothes, which he only wore to annoy his mom who kept on sending them to him in hopes he'd find high-society events to attend.

I also found out he had graduated top of his class, gave his parents his Business degree, and left for San Diego the next day.

Maybe there was more in common between us than I thought, despite our age and background difference.

"Will you tell me about your Uncle Ted? You said he saved your life."

I stared at Aiden. There were so many ways I could tell this story, including the one I'd told Mike when we met. But when I opened my mouth, nothing came out.

Aiden held my hand and took it to his lips, keeping it there.

"Aiden, I...what I'm going to tell you could change the way you see me or feel about me."

"You're wrong. Nothing you can tell me will change how I see the man in front of me, nothing."

He sounded so sure of himself, of me.

A tiny moment in time was all it would take. I took a deep breath.

"I shot a man when I was twenty years old."

"What did he do to deserve it?"

I sat up.

"What? What kind of question is that? No one deserves to die at the hands of another person."

Aiden pulled my arm to lie down again.

"Tell me your story and I will prove you wrong."

"How can you do that? You weren't there?"

"No, but I know you, Slade."

I put my hand on his face, feeling his warm skin. How could I tell him he didn't know me at all?

"Remember when I told you that I left my parents' place to keep them safe?"

"Yes."

"I'd been a member of the club for a year when the president died in an accident. He was succeeded by the vice president. For some reason, that guy didn't like me. I overheard someone say once that the reason I'd been voted in was because the president thought my skills with the bikes would be handy in the club. The vice president disagreed."

"So, when he became president, things got hard for you?"

"Yeah, weird stuff started happening around me. Dead animals were dropped on my foster parents' doorstep. I'd wake up with shit smeared all over my bedroom window. But the worst was when those things happened even when I wasn't at home. I figured it would stop if I moved."

"Did it?"

"Yeah. I rented out a room in a house with some students because it was cheap. Same stuff kept happening, so I had to move again."

"Did you tell anyone about it?"

"I didn't know who to tell. The police wouldn't do anything, and the new president of the club hated my guts for no apparent reason. He did let me stay at the clubhouse until I found a new place."

Aiden scrunched up his eyes. "I'm not gonna like this, am I? I know you're here and you're okay, but I don't like where the story is going."

"I was attacked on my first night. A group of men beat the crap out of me and left me there with broken ribs, a bleeding eye, and lots of bruises. The guys started an investigation, thinking it was a rival club that had come in looking for revenge on some stuff our club did."

"Was it?"

"I thought it was at the time. Weeks later, I was asleep when I heard noise in the house. I'd gotten a gun after the beating because I was too scared of being on my own. When the door to my room opened, I pretended to be asleep. The first thing I saw was a gun pointing at me. Everything happened too fast. I shot my gun and the attacker fell on the floor. It was like everything was silent, then there was this loud noise, and then silence again. I was so terrified of even turning the lights on, I ran out of the room and called my old neighbor. He called an ambulance and told me to get out of the house."

AIDEN

The story out of Slade's lips was the stuff of movies and books, not real life.

"Who was your attacker?" I asked.

"The son of the new president. I shot him in the neck. He's paralyzed for the rest of his life... Aiden, I didn't even aim. I just shot."

Slade's voice had been steady, up to the moment when he finally broke down.

"I have so many regrets," he said as his eyes filled with tears.

"You acted in self-defense. If you hadn't shot, you would be the one who was dead. So how did Ted get to save your life?"

"My neighbor gave me the signal to run because the president was out for revenge. He said I'd killed his son and needed to pay with my life."

"But he didn't die."

"No, but for a biker, being unable to ride is as good as being dead. So many times I wished I'd aimed at a leg or an arm, or that instead of a gun I'd had a baseball bat or something. I don't know. Anything but that fucking gun."

He shook his head. I wanted so much to take that pain away, but I had a feeling that Slade needed to finish the story.

"What happened next?"

"I ran, but every time I got a job and a new place to stay, I'd find myself being followed, getting threats in the mail. They were tracking my social security number."

"If they wanted to kill you they could have done it from afar without warning."

"The bastard wanted me to be scared, to keep running for my life until he was tired of playing. This went on for four years until I went to the police. I promised I'd tell them anything they needed to know about the club if they helped me hide somewhere safe. I was so scared that even if they had put me in jail I would have thanked them. The officer I spoke to lost his brother to gang crime, so he took all the information he could from me and gave me an address in Atlanta."

"Ted?"

For the first time since Slade started his story he smiled, a genuine happy smile.

"I was gathering enough courage to go in and speak to Ted when Mike saw me. His smile was infectious, and if I'm honest, that's what made me cross the road. Someone who smiled like that couldn't have a difficult life, couldn't know what I knew. I craved that. He was like those jam-filled doughnuts. You have one and then another. But by the third you think you're gonna die, so you wait a little longer and then you can eat another one. And when the bag is empty, you go buy more. Because who wouldn't want to live for jam-filled doughnuts?"

My heart filled with hope for the young guy who'd gone through so much and finally found his little piece of heaven.

"There was a cost to all that though. Ted knew about me, but Mike couldn't. Within a few weeks I had a new name and social security number. I was a new person. It took me exactly six months to ask Mike to marry me, even when it wasn't legal to do it. We actually never really got married, even though we used the terms marriage and divorce, we didn't do it officially."

"Why?"

"I don't know. I always held back. The longer I lived my new life, the longer the lie chased me. Mike knew I loved him, but there was something missing."

He didn't need to tell me anything else. The time for talking was over.

I ran my fingers softly down his face, collecting the few tears that left his eyes, stroked his soft beard, and then pressed my lips against his.

"Slade," I whispered.

"Yeah?"

"I'm still here."

"I'm still me."

"You are, as am I."

For the rest of the night, Slade took solace in my body. I was his safe place because he was mine. I'd decided I was going to keep him because anything else just didn't seem like an option to me.

When I opened my eyes the next morning, Slade wasn't in bed. I knew I was a cuddler, so it was a testament to how much he wore me out the night before that I didn't feel him leave.

I got up to use the bathroom, and when I came out, he was coming back into the room with coffee and a bag.

"Morning. I got us some pastries. Figured we should eat something, even though I'm not really hungry."

I walked toward him and smiled when he opened his arms for me instantly.

"Thank you. You're right, we should eat something.'

The hospital was a short drive away from the hotel. The closer we got, the more fidgety Slade became. He was clearly anxious to find out more about his uncle's health, and I suspected also nervous to see his ex-husband.

Mike was nothing like what I'd expected. Physically, if Slade was a silver-fox, Mike was a total bear. He had shiny eyes, a thick beard, and a friendly smile.

"Mike this is Aiden, my..."

"Friend," I said, interrupting Slade. "Nice to meet you."

Mike held out his hand. "Likewise."

There was an awkward pause until Slade said, "Can we see Ted?"

"Of course. I'm afraid it's family only," Mike said, looking at me. I couldn't tell if he was apologetic or not.

"That's okay, I expected that. I'll wait for you here."

Slade seemed a little lost, so I stepped into his arms, hugging him tight. I didn't care who Mike thought I was to Slade. Friend was an accurate term and friends supported friends in difficult times.

"You'll be okay. And if you're not, that's okay too. I'll be here. I promise."

He nodded and disappeared into a corridor with Mike.

I took a deep breath. The nurses station was quiet, so I thought I'd chance my luck. Slade had told me last night he took Ted's surname when he got his new ID, so I approached with a smile and fingers crossed.

"Hi, I was wondering if you could help me, please."

"I'm afraid I'm limited in the information I can give out if that's what you're needing."

I smiled at her. "You get that a lot, do you?"

"Yup."

"I don't want any specific information. I just...my friend has gone to see his uncle. They're very close. All I want to know is...is he likely to be very upset when he comes out of there later?"

She gave me a sympathetic smile. "What's the patient's name?"

"Ted Warren."

She tapped on her computer and seemed to be reading some information.

I already knew the news before she even spoke because her eyes spelled it out.

"There's a cafeteria down that hall. Buy a bottle of water. Next door there's a small store that sells essentials. Get a pack of tissues. You might not need them, but..."

"Thank you so much."

A few minutes later I was back in the waiting room. It was hard to guess if Slade staying in the ward too long meant good or bad news.

I nearly jumped out of my skin when my phone buzzed in my pocket.

Richard's name was on the screen.

What the hell?

I declined the call, but a few seconds later, he rang again.

"Hello?

"Aiden... Hi, how are you?"

"Surprised to hear from you if I'm honest."

This was so not the time for this.

"Yeah, I'm sorry. I wanted to get in touch but...well, we didn't part on the best of terms."

Gee, I wonder why.

"Richard, I'm busy at the moment. How can I help you?"

"When are you back in town?"

"What...what do you mean?"

"I stopped by the apartment and you weren't there. I'd love to take you out when you're back."

Something didn't feel right about this. Why was he at the apartment?

Calm down, Aiden. He can't get in. He doesn't live there anymore.

"I don't know when I'm going to be back, and I'm also not available to go out with you."

"Why? Don't tell me you found yourself some loser to fuck around with."

My nerves reached such a high just from hearing his voice that I laughed aloud.

"First of all, Richard, my life is none of your business. When I say I can't see you, take it at face value. Good—"

"Wait."

"What?"

I was losing patience now. Slade had been in the ward for almost three hours and I needed to know if he was okay.

"I'm going to send you a little gift. Just watch it and call me after."

He ended the call, and a moment later I received a message with a video attachment.

I opened the video. As soon as it started playing I turned the volume down. It was footage of my apartment. Someone was taking the camera from the living room through the hall and into my bedroom.

As soon as I saw the next frame I got up from the chair and ran to the nearest bathroom.

I barely had time to close the door behind me before I emptied the contents of my stomach into the toilet.

No, this could not be happening.

SLADE

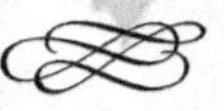

The man on the hospital bed wasn't Ted. The man on the hospital bed looked frail, pale, far too slim, and like someone whose life was hanging by a thread.

I'd watched him sleep for the last hour. He hadn't moved, but the machines around him beeped reassuringly. Mike had tried to talk, but I couldn't.

Maybe that was the last time I'd see Ted. Silence was what I needed. Silence and Aiden.

I'd have given anything to have him there with me, but he couldn't be, so I had to focus on the knowledge he was down the corridor waiting for me.

"How long?" I asked when staring at Ted didn't give me the answers I needed.

"The doctors don't know. The cancer spread to his vital organs and he's too weak to have any more treatment."

"Why didn't you tell me?"

"Would you have come? You left as if what I did was the worst thing someone could have done to another person. I didn't kill anyone, Slade. I cheated, and only because our relationship had been dead for years. Did you ever think what your distance was doing to us? To me?"

Anger bubbled inside me.

"Don't you dare make this about us. This has nothing to do with you and me."

"Oh really? Then how many times have you called Uncle Ted since you left? The man gave you his name. He treated you like a son."

"Boys."

Ted's voice was weak, but even now he was able to convey the warning tone he'd used on us so many times when we hadn't been able to agree on something.

"Will you make me rise from the dead to stop your stupid arguments?"

"Hey, Ted." I stepped closer to the bed and took his hand in mine. He squeezed it tight, his hand trembling.

"Hey, son, you lookin' good."

I smiled. "I wish I could say the same about you. You look like shit."

He laughed and then coughed until he got his breathing back again.

"Mike, will you give us a moment?" Ted asked.

Mike frowned at me. I knew he wanted to argue.

"I promise not to die in the next ten minutes," Ted said when Mike didn't move.

"Jesus Christ, Ted. This isn't funny."

"I disagree. Now scoot, I need a word with my boy."

"Why do I feel like I'm going to have my ass handed to me?" I said as Mike stepped out of the room.

Ted smiled, his eyes scanning my face as if he were trying to remember what I looked like.

"I'm sorry I didn't—"

He raised his hand to stop me.

"Son, when time is in short supply there's no need for apologies or regrets. It is what it is."

I nodded.

"Tell me something, son. Did I help you? Did I do the right thing?"

Tears ran down my face, and I didn't even bother to stop them or pretend they weren't there. Sometimes it was okay to think you're too fucking old to care about crying in front of someone else.

"Ted, you gave me a future. You could have said no to your friend, and I'll never understand why you'd put your life at risk for a nobody like me, but there isn't enough gratitude in the world for what you did to me."

"Let me tell you a little story. Before I married my darling Rose, I was a bit of a player. I got my first bike at fifteen, and in those days, you could do what you liked. So I saved up some money to go traveling the country. My mom and dad weren't too pleased, but I promised I'd come back and take over the business. So, at eighteen, I left. Traveled all the way to the west coast and then followed the ocean north. You're staring at a wrinkly old man now, but I tell you, I was quite the catch back then. Never had any problem getting girls or boys."

He stopped to catch his breath.

"You're bi?"

"Don't be so surprised, son. Remember Walter? The army friend who lived with me for a few years?"

I laughed. "He wasn't just your army friend?"

"That man saved me from spending the rest of my life grieving for my Rose."

I couldn't believe it. Walter had lived with Ted for five years and there was never any indication they were more than just friends. Considering Mike and I were together, I didn't think coming out would have been an issue. Then again, Ted had always been quite private with his life.

"Anyway, back to the early days. I met Nico at a party. We hit it off immediately and he came traveling with me. We both knew our relationship was only temporary because I had to come back to Atlanta, and he had to get back to Seattle. We parted on friendly terms and kept writing to each other for years after that. He became my best friend. He knew Rose and I struggled to conceive, and I lost all hope of becoming a father when she was taken from me too young."

Ted told me the story as if he was recounting someone else's life. How could he be so measured when inside my heart was breaking with each word he spoke?

"He gave you a son," I said. My words choked as I said them. "He gave me to you."

"That's right. It wasn't the intention, I guess. He knew I ran a business and could use a hand, and he trusted me to keep your secret and keep you safe. You became my son when you told my horndog of a nephew to take a hike unless you could tell me about you two. That was the kind of respect you showed a parent. That was when you became my son."

I stood up from the chair and hugged Ted. I'd always looked up to him like a son, but I didn't know he'd felt the same way. Why was I losing him now?

He stroked my hair, and we stayed like that for a moment until my tears stopped.

"I know Mike did wrong by you, and I know you had secrets to keep from him, but..."

"Ted, we can't get back together, you know that, right?"

He smiled. "I know. It's too late now. Can I ask you something? Will you keep in touch with him? Since you left he hasn't been with anyone. He's lonely, and I think he's still in love with you. I'm not asking for more than a friendly hand. Don't let him lose himself to work."

"I promise, Ted. I do miss him and his annoying habits and terrible taste in music. Does he still play Britney Spears in the garage while he works?"

"He's graduated to Beyoncé."

I snorted.

"And how about you? Your business doing well? Mike searched for you on the internet and said you have a vintage bike shop and garage?"

"Yeah. Business is doing well, and I love Connecticut."

Ted closed his eyes for a moment, his face looked tired all of a sudden, and I wondered if he was ready to sleep again.

"Let me call Mike back, okay?"

"Just one thing, son. Don't let the past drag behind you like a bad smell. We all have pasts. I know you couldn't have done anything about Mike, but you're still young. If there's another chance out there waiting for you, take it."

I thought about Aiden and the conversation we'd had last night when I'd told him everything. Ted was right.

"Ted, my second chance is on the other side of that door a few yards away, waiting for me. He's wonderful, and you'll get to meet him soon."

He nodded and closed his eyes.

I called Mike back into the room.

"So I guess that's it now. We can't fight and you have to be my friend," he said.

"You got the pep talk too?"

Mike smiled. His brown eyes looked at me with the same love they always held, but also more.

I walked over and hugged him. He hugged me back. We were the same height, but Mike always felt like he was bigger to me.

"You still give the best hugs," I said.

"Remember that."

Ted opened his eyes again and raised both his hands. We stood on either side of his bed, holding his hands, and then reached out for each other too.

"Now that's better," he said, his speech a little slurred. "Rose, honey, I'm on my way. There better be cherry pie."

He closed his eyes, and a minute later, the machines Ted

was connected to gave us the warning he was no longer with us.

The nurses ran into the room to silence the beeping noise and do what they needed to do. Mike and I held each other as we said one final goodbye to the man that had been a father to both of us.

AIDEN

*I*f I was writing my life as it was, I'd have the presence of mind to know I was in shock. But I wasn't writing it, I was living it, and when you're living your life, you don't stop to consider your feelings, your actions, the bigger picture.

So yeah, the moment I saw Slade walk down the corridor hand in hand with Mike, I pocketed my phone and ran toward him.

He opened his arms for me and held me tight. I felt his tears on my neck. There was nothing I could say in that moment, so I let him cry as I ran my hands up and down his back.

When he finally stopped, I cleaned the tears with a tissue and handed him the bottle of water.

Slade smiled and drank most of the water in one go.

"I'm so sorry for your loss, Mike," I said and ran my hand up his arm. He looked very shaken too.

"Would you...would you come home with me? There's a few things Ted said he wanted you to have," Mike said to Slade.

"I'll go back to the hotel and pick you up later when you're ready," I said.

"No. You're coming with us."

Mike nodded. He didn't seem upset that I was tagging along, but I still felt like I was being assessed.

We followed Mike's car in silence, which put me a little on edge. My phone burned in my pocket, buzzing every so often, but I ignored it.

I looked at Slade, who was staring out of the window, lost in thought.

"Hey," I said gently.

"Hey," he replied. I glanced at him when we hit a red traffic light and he was staring at me.

I took his hand and lifted it to my lips, kissing his palm.

"It's been a while, huh?" I said.

"Yeah. These streets are so different now, but they're also the same."

Ted's place was like I'd imagined. The garage was shut, but from the size of the metal gates, it was much bigger than Slade's, though there was no shop attached to it. We followed Mike to a door on the side which led to an indoor staircase. At the top there were two doors, one on either side.

Mike opened the door to the left, but I noticed Slade staring at the door on the right.

It was strange being in the house of a man I hadn't met and that had just passed away.

The place was very tidy and didn't have much inside.

"He started getting rid of stuff when he got the terminal diagnosis," Mike said. "He said there was no point in keeping old crap as he put it."

"He got rid of his chair too?" Slade asked.

"No, that's at our place, um...my place. He moved in with me a few months ago."

Mike picked up a box and took us to his place, which as it turned out was the door opposite Ted's.

I felt like I was intruding in Slade's old life as I followed them into Mike's place. There were photos of them all over the walls.

Two young guys with their arms around each other, clearly so much in love. There were photos of the beach, mountains, viewpoints. It looked like they'd traveled and enjoyed their life together.

"Um, can I make myself useful? I can make coffee or get some water, if you like?" I asked. They were both on the couch with the box on the coffee table in front of them.

"Thank you, Aiden, coffee would be nice, actually. The kitchen is through there, everything is easy to find."

I nodded and walked toward the corridor leading to the kitchen, busying myself with the coffee machine. My phone buzzed again. I took it out just in time to see the screen go dark as the battery died. That was probably for the best.

I needed to keep going, keep focusing on Slade and what he needed. Mike too. What I saw on my phone had to have an explanation, but now wasn't the time to seek it.

As I waited for the coffee to brew, I inspected a notice board next to the fridge. There were cards with medical appointments, takeout menus, and some photos. All of them included Slade.

Was Mike holding on to Slade? Had he not moved on?

We spent the rest of the day with Mike. I mostly watched as they remembered Ted as they went through old photos and memories. I could see how Slade and Mike had been so suited to each other.

Mike was, for the lack of a better term, a big teddy bear of a man, with his sparkly eyes and friendly personality. He really didn't match the actions of a man who'd cheated on his husband.

After dinner I offered to wash up the dishes while they put all the photos away.

I was drying them when Mike came in the kitchen.

"Hey," I said. "All okay out there?"

"Yeah, he's just in the bathroom...um, Aiden...I'm...I don't know how to say this, but I hope you love him as much as he loves you."

"What do you mean, he doesn't..."

My heart raced. Okay, I'd hoped that was the case, but that was before my phone call this morning. Before the video. I still hadn't handled that. How would Slade react when he found out?

"I've known that man half my life. I always knew there was something he wasn't telling me about himself. There was something missing in our relationship. My uncle always defended Slade, so I learned to accept that something happened in his past that I couldn't know about. But I can tell he's told you because he looks at you like you're his lifeline. He leans on you more than he ever leaned on me. So if you know his truth, you know how much that means."

I put the dishcloth on the counter and hugged Mike.

"You're a good man, Mike."

"Eh, I have my moments."

"Will you be okay after he leaves?"

"I'll make do."

We ended up checking out of the hotel and staying with Mike for a few days until the funeral.

The ordeal of putting his uncle to rest was too much for Slade, so whenever he wasn't helping Mike with stuff, he was asleep.

I ended up finding Mike and I had more in common than just Slade, and before we left I made him promise to visit Slade in Chester Falls at some point.

He gave me a pointed stare when it sounded as though I might not be around then, but I deflected.

When Slade had been asleep, and with my phone's battery fully charged, I'd finally seen the whole video. I'd had to hide in the bathroom so I wouldn't disturb Slade.

I'd also read the messages from Richard. *I want to see you. When will you be back? Don't ignore me, dammit. Aiden, we have a history together. Did you like the video we made, sweetie? You loved being a dirty little whore for me, didn't you?*

I stopped being able to read more of the messages through the tears in my eyes.

There was no way out of this. What if he went public with the video? He'd been clever enough so that while I'd been fully exposed, his face wasn't visible. The person on the video could literally be anyone. Which meant he was holding the cards in my life. Again.

The closer we were to Chester Falls, the more anxious I got. I still hadn't decided what I was going to do about Richard. I knew I had to call him, but I was terrified of doing it.

"Hey, you're a million miles away," Slade said, taking my hand and lacing our fingers together over his thigh.

"Just thinking."

"About your book?"

"Um, yeah..."

"Let me know if there's anything else I can help you with for your research. Liam texted me to say the parts that went off to be powder-coated are back."

It seemed that as my anxiety spiked, Slade's seemed to disappear, so I let him believe I'd simply been thinking about my book.

When we arrived at his place, I made excuses that I had stuff to catch up on and told him to spend some time with Harley. He'd looked at me funny but didn't argue, especially since he did have a business to run and had been away for almost a week.

As if Richard could guess I was on my own, his name appeared on the screen of my phone.

I straightened my back, hoping it would give me extra courage, and answered the call.

"What do you want?"

"I told you, baby. I want you to come home. To me. Where you belong."

"What's the point? I don't love you and you don't love me. You know I can't get married without a prenup, so what's your goal?

"Oh, honey, a relationship is much more than loving someone. It's about companionship, it's about the things we can do for each other." His voice grated on me. How had I never noticed how whiny he sounded? Oh yeah, because he'd manipulated me into loving him.

"You mean you want access to my money."

He gasped. "Honey, I'm shocked you'd say that. This is about us taking care of each other. Your mother agrees we should give our relationship another try."

My heart sank. He'd been speaking to my parents?

After being around Aiden for a whole week, it was strange not having him around. My apartment felt empty, and I was at a loss for what to do.

He'd seemed eager to go home on his own, which after the week we'd had didn't surprise me, and that was why I hadn't pressed the matter.

Aiden had gotten along with Mike better than I'd expected. Well, I hadn't expected them to get along at all.

Since my talk with Ted, and then after going to Mike's place, I'd noticed certain things about Mike.

He'd lost a little of his spark and there was no indication in the apartment that he'd had anyone over at all. In fact, visiting the apartment now was more or less like stepping into our old life.

Had Mike been on his own since we split? Maybe I'd been unfair to him when we spoke that first time. It didn't matter, we'd parted on good terms and I had a feeling we'd stay in touch.

If that had been Ted's last wish, then he'd succeeded.

But I couldn't shake the feeling that there was something up with Aiden. I'd noticed he'd been quieter than usual.

Was he having doubts about us? Was coming to Atlanta with me too much? After all, he was young, and guys his age didn't often have to face the mortality of a loved one, even if he didn't know Ted. Or maybe it was all the stuff I'd offloaded on him.

I ran my fingers through my hair, walking up and down my living room. He'd said he was there...here, he'd said he was here for me. But what if he'd said it because he knew we were about to visit a dying man? What if he was trying to make me feel better?

There was a knock on my door. Was Aiden back? I ran to it so fast, I nearly tripped on my feet.

When I opened the door, I was faced with the last person I ever thought I'd see again.

"Hey, Doc, you gonna invite me in?"

The respect for a fellow club member was so ingrained in me, even after all these years, that all I could do was step aside and let him in.

"Nice place. I see you're in shock, so let's clarify some things first. I'm alone. I come in peace, just to see a friend."

I knew he wouldn't harm me, he'd been one of the nicest guys at the club, but the thought that they were still out there and maybe looking for me made my blood run cold.

"Kickstand," I finally said.

"Once a Kickstand, always a Kickstand, right? Although it's President Kickstand now."

He turned around to show me his club patch. *The Lost Puppies*.

"You're not with the club?" I asked.

"Nah, man, the club disbanded after the police got their hands on the president and found out he was involved in a load of illegal shit. Haven't seen any of them for years. Last I heard, half of them had died either from illness or less natural causes, if you know what I mean."

I shook my head. "I can't believe you're here."

"If I'm honest, me neither."

"Let me get us something to drink. You riding?" I asked.

"Yeah. If you have beer, I'll take one and a glass of water."

I grabbed a couple of beers from the fridge and went back to the living room where Kickstand was inspecting my bookshelf.

"Damn. I wanna make fun of you, but I did a stint in prison a few years back and started reading to pass the time. This A. Lawton guy is good."

I smiled. "That he is. So, tell me, Kick...I don't even know what your real name is."

"Travis."

"Travis, how did you find me?"

"I should be offended that you didn't recognize me, but then again you were with a guy that had the tightest ass I've ever seen, so I don't blame you for not noticing."

I ignored the way he spoke about Aiden and tried to think instead about where I'd been with Aiden that Travis would have been too.

"The roadside bar. Was that you...your club?"

"Yeah. I wanted to approach you then, but I didn't know what kind of life you have now, or who you're involved with, so I took your license plate and did some digging around to find you."

I laughed. "Haven't been involved with anything since I escaped that hellhole. I ride solo these days."

"Yeah, I gathered. Your shop looks great, by the way.'

"Thanks. So tell me about your club. President? Who did you accidentally kill to become president of anything?"

He raised a brow and took a sip of his beer.

"Fuck you, Doc. No one was hurt in my quest to be president of The Lost Puppies."

I nearly spluttered my beer all over the couch.

"Okay, please call me Slade. Doc died a long time ago, and

I'm an independent now, so there's no formality there. What I want to know is...Lost Puppies? Really?"

"I'll spare you my life story, but we're mainly a child support charity. We organize runs to raise money for kids that need help with medical care, education tools, and we run a Big Biker, Little Biker group for kids without a male role model."

I had no words. I always saw my past as something ugly, rotten, evil. Everyone and everything was bad. Even when I knew I'd met good people, such as my foster parents and my neighbor, they were linked to that time in my life and became mixed in with the darkness.

Maybe I wasn't the only one in the darkness. And maybe just like I'd found something good to hold on to, Ted and Mike, other guys had too.

"How did you get into the club?"

"I married into it."

"Congrats, man."

He shook his head.

"Oh, fuck, I'm sorry."

"Yeah, lost Sam going on ten years ago."

"I'm so sorry, Travis."

He finished his beer and drank the full glass of water straight away.

"I look back sometimes and wonder at how many lifetimes I've lived already, you know? How many life-changing decisions I've made. How cursed I felt and how lucky I was. Still am."

Wasn't that the truth?

"I know how that feels more than you know, brother."

He peeked at his watch and stood up. "I better get going. Sorry to drop on your doorstep unannounced like this. When I saw you, I...I don't know. I don't have great memories of that time, but I always thought you were a good guy, and if life taught me anything, it was to hold on to the good guys."

I stepped into his space and gave him a hug.

"Thank you, Travis. I am glad you came by. Let's keep in touch."

After he left, I had a sudden rush of energy come over me. I was dying to see Aiden, touch him, make love to him, tell him I was so ridiculously in love with him. I wanted to beg him to move to Chester Falls, or hell, I'd move to San Diego.

Was there anything more worthy in life than pursuing this? No.

I'd lost so much in my life already. But I'd also gained so much. It was time to focus on the good stuff. And Aiden was my good stuff.

But after being thrust into my life over the last week, Aiden deserved some time to himself. I'd give him tonight, and then tomorrow I'd sweep him off his feet or kidnap him and tie him to my bed. Potato, potahto.

I spent the rest of the day cleaning the apartment, catching up with my laundry, and even cooked a nice meal for myself, which I ate after I had a long, hot shower and trimmed my beard.

After dinner I settled on the couch with one of the books I'd gotten at the book fair and hadn't read yet. I hadn't even gotten to the end of the first chapter when my phone rang.

I smiled when I saw Aiden's name pop up.

"Hey."

"Hi...Slade. Um, I'm sorry to do this to you last minute, but I have to go back to San Diego. I can't help you finish the bike. I'm so sorry."

What? No. No. No.

"Aiden, what's wrong? You don't sound like yourself. Let me come over there."

"No! I'm fine, honestly. I just have stuff I need to attend to. I haven't been home for nearly a month, so..."

"Can I come with you? You shouldn't drive all the way on your own."

"No, please, Slade, just..." He let out a breath on the other side.

Was this it? Were we done, just like that, with no explanation?

"Aid, please. I know the last week was tough. All the stuff I told you, and then Ted and meeting Mike, but—"

"Slade." He said my name as if it were final. "I'm sorry."

He hung up, which was as good as sticking a knife right through my heart and twisting it.

AIDEN

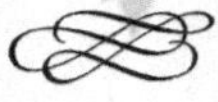

*I*t took me a whole hour after hanging up on Slade to pull myself off the floor where I'd sat down crying. I'd promised I'd be there for him, and I was breaking that promise.

I needed to get to San Diego and face Richard. Maybe I could convince him to delete the video.

Even as the thought crossed my mind, I knew it was pointless. He probably already had a bunch of copies. He could delete the video, but I'd never trust that there wasn't another copy out there.

Maybe he just wanted money, maybe I could pay him off. If he'd been after me just for the money, surely that would be it, right? I'd pay him off and he'd go away.

Except he could come back over and over again. I would never be free of him.

A new sob of desperation ran through me.

"Come on, Aiden. Pick yourself up. You need to figure this shit out. Do I fly, or do I drive?"

If I took a flight, I'd get there faster, but I'd still need to drive my car to the airport and then I'd have no way to get it. If

I drove, it would take me a week to get to the other side of the country.

I picked up my phone and opened the messaging app.

Aiden: I need to drive home. It'll take me a week.

Richard: A week? Where are you? Timbuktu?

Aiden: I'm on the East Coast.

Richard: Oh, visiting your little friends, are you? I suppose since you're coming home to me, I'll wait.

Aiden: Thank you.

Two hours later I had the car packed up, saving for some last-minute items, and I'd called the parents of the apartment owner to let them know I'd be leaving in the morning.

There was one last thing, I needed to speak to Wren. It wasn't fair to leave without any warning, but it was already too late to drop by his place. I messaged him for a run early in the morning, which was met with a GIF of a cat yawning, but since he didn't flat out say no, I assumed he'd be here.

Going for a run on very little sleep was a bad idea, but since good ideas were in short supply these days, I'd have to suck it up.

"Why are we running so early? Have you killed Slade with your energetic lovemaking?" Wren said, using the steps outside my building to stretch his legs.

"No, I wasn't with him last night."

"Ahh, too horny to sleep. Gotcha."

We started with a slow jog to warm up. We usually picked up our pace once we were on the forest trail.

"Tom and I have some news," he said.

"You finally got him pregnant after all this time trying?"

"Never have I ever been so glad to be with a guy. We can try all we want. And we do try a lot," he said.

"Is it something you want?"

We ran in silence for a moment, picking up the pace a little. It was harder to speak, but we'd been doing this for a long time and needing oxygen had never stopped us from managing a conversation.

"Yeah. We want to have the wedding first, go on a honeymoon, and then when we're back, we'll start looking into surrogacy."

"That's great. Congrats. Was that your news?"

"No, we have a wedding date."

"Wow, when?"

"December twentieth."

"This year?"

"Yeah."

"Okay, I'm sure I can come back for that."

I was so focused on breathing that I didn't realize Wren had stopped completely.

"What do you mean, you'll come back for it?"

"You know I don't live here, right?"

"Yeah, but with Slade being here, I thought..."

I took a deep breath and went for it. Pull it off like a Band-Aid and get it over with.

"I'm leaving today."

"What?"

Wren's voice was so loud that some birds in nearby trees took flight.

"What happened? Why so soon?"

"It's not really that soon, is it? I've been here for three weeks."

"But you went to Atlanta with Slade. I thought you guys were—"

"Having fun. That's what we were doing. Yes, I was there for him at a difficult time, but it doesn't mean that he'll want a relationship with me. And I have things to do in San Diego, so..."

"I don't buy it."

"You don't need to. It is what it is," I said, hoping this would put the conversation to an end.

He resumed the run, so I thought we were done, until he stopped again.

"Are you in love with him?"

Of course I'm fucking in love with him. That's what I wanted to say, but what I said instead was, "He was a good fuck."

Classy, Aiden. Very classy.

Wren pulled my arm with such force that I thought it was going to detach from my body and wrapped his arms around me.

He didn't say anything for a long time, just stayed there, in the middle of the forest, hugging me. And the longer he did it, the bigger the lump in my throat grew.

"Fuck you, Wren, for making me cry. I'm going to miss you, you fucking motherfucker."

"Since when did you develop such a potty mouth, Aiden Lawton?" he joked, but his hold on me didn't let up. "I don't know what's going on, Aid, but I love you and Tom loves you, and so do the rest of the guys. We'll miss you."

All I could do was nod against him.

"And you better throw me a kick-ass bachelor party."

"What?"

"Please don't insult me by being surprised that I'm asking you to be my best man."

I laughed. "I'd be honored."

We finished the run, and I promised to be in touch soon.

I stopped in Ohio for the night. Exhausted and hungry, I grabbed a burger from a local bar and went straight to bed in a roadside motel.

I had another four days of this until I was home. Not that San Diego or my apartment felt like home anymore. It was more like I was heading to a prison sentence.

Throughout the week, Richard kept texting and asking where I was. I ignored as many of them as I could without setting him off. The drive also made me reflect a lot on my relationship with Richard.

I came to terms that it had been an abusive relationship.

How had I not noticed how we only had sex when he wanted? How I always paid for everything? How he'd put me down if my book didn't hit the charts on release day? How he seemed to be purposefully noisy when I needed silence to write, and then berate me for not hitting my word count?

I tried to keep as many of those thoughts at bay because they made me cry, and I couldn't drive if I was crying.

By the third day, anxiety was my constant companion. Were there more videos?

I tried to remember how many times he'd asked to blindfold me during sex, saying we needed to be more adventurous in bed. Our relationship would last longer if we had fun in bed.

I'd never had fun in those times. I wasn't even able to orgasm. But he seemed to enjoy it, so I did it for an easy life. How had I not seen the signs?

When I saw the road sign for San Diego, my mind was in such a state of confusion that I wasn't sure if I was happy, sad, or afraid to have arrived.

At least I could take a long bath and rest in my own bed before I had to face Richard.

I tried not to think of Slade, but that was a failed attempt. Every mile away from him was like a part of my heart was being shredded and left on the side of the road.

I would call him soon and apologize properly. He deserved that much. Maybe Mike would visit him at some point, and they would rekindle their love.

That thought made me feel sick, and not just because thinking of them together made me jealous. I knew deep down Slade and Mike had had their time and it had ended.

What made me feel sick was the thought of Slade either settling for a half-love or being alone forever.

By the time I pulled in front of my apartment, I was beyond exhausted. I knew I'd pushed the last few hundred miles. I really should have stopped another night, but I just wanted my own bed.

I didn't bother with anything else in the car other than my laptop bag, which had my wallet and phone inside. I locked the car and dragged my tired legs up the stairs to the front door.

My stomach jumped when I saw a figure standing by the door. My eyes were dry from the contacts, so I rubbed my them and looked up again.

"Slade? What are you doing—"

SLADE

"*I* love you. I love you. I love you."

Aiden threw himself at me, saying the words over and over again. I wasn't even sure he was conscious that he was saying it. But damn, even if I lost my hearing, I'd still remember it for the rest of my life. All I could do was hope that I would hear this for the rest of my life.

"Well, that was easier than I thought," I said into his hair, kissing his head as he lowered his voice to a whisper but never stopped saying he loved me.

"Baby, let me take you upstairs," I said. He nodded and leaned into me as he got out the key to the door. I grabbed the handle of my suitcase and let him guide us.

Aiden's apartment was enormous. Most of it seemed open plan with a corridor on the opposite end to the front door.

"Is that the way to your bedroom?"

He nodded.

We dropped the bags by the couch and walked to the bedroom.

Aiden seemed to be in a zombie-like state. He was probably overly tired and had just stayed alert long enough to make it home. The thought that he could have had an accident made my blood run cold, but he was here and unharmed, and that was all that mattered.

When I found the bathroom attached to his room I helped him out of his clothes and turned the shower on. It was quite warm inside the apartment, so I opened a few windows to get a breeze through and some fresh air.

When the water was warm enough, I undressed and pulled Aiden into the shower with me.

"Are you okay?" I asked.

"Yes. Are you really here?"

"I am, baby. And in case you're wondering, I love you too."

He started crying into my chest.

"It's okay, baby. I'll keep repeating it until the words are all you can remember forever."

I grabbed his shampoo and lathered it in my hand before running it over his hair, massaging his scalp. Aiden looked like he was hanging by a thread, but he was still standing up on his own so that was a good thing.

As soon as we were both washed, I helped him get dried and then carried him over to the bedroom.

"I'm not a princess," he slurred.

"No, baby, but I'm going to treat you like one until you're feeling better."

"No pillows..."

"You don't want pillows or you do?"

"More pillows, your pillows."

I chuckled. His closet held two extra, so I grabbed them and placed them behind him before I settled against him, pulling the covers over us.

Aiden was asleep even before I finished tucking him up properly. I wrapped my arms around him, feeling at peace for the first time since he'd left me in my apartment.

Sleep claimed me shortly after.

I woke up to Aiden's barely coherent moans. He was

moving, but without enough force that he'd hurt me or himself.

"No, please, don't do it. Please..."

"Shh, baby, it's okay," I whispered, hoping he'd wake up of his own accord.

"No, no, it's not. Don't do it."

I had no clue what he was dreaming about, but it didn't sound pleasant.

"Aiden, sweetheart. Can you wake up for me?" I ran my hands through his hair until he stopped moving and his eyes opened slowly.

"Slade?"

"There you are," I said, smiling. "My beautiful, brown-eyed boy."

"No," he screamed, sitting up in bed. "No, you can t be here. Oh my god, what if he sees you?"

He scrambled off the bed to a chest of drawers, taking out underwear and then a pair of sweatpants and a T-shirt.

I got up and went over to him. When I turned him around, his eyes were full of tears.

"Aiden, what's going on? You're worrying the hell out of me."

I'd known something was wrong with Aiden even before Wren and Tom had turned up at my doorstep with blazing guns and threats of the make-it-right-or-lose-your-balls kind.

So I'd spent a whole night tossing and turning, trying to analyze every conversation we'd had, every time we'd been together, and as a last resort, I'd called Mike.

After all we'd been with him almost a week, so maybe he'd seen something in Aiden, or maybe they'd talked. Mike had not just suggested but pointed right out that we were in love with each other but neither had actually said those words.

And *that* was what I thought was wrong.

But the state Aiden was in meant there had to be more to him rushing to San Diego.

I ran over to the living room to grab some clothes from my suitcase and rushed back to the bedroom.

Aiden was sitting on the edge of his bed with his head down. I sat next to him.

"What happened, Aiden?"

"Richard...Richard called me when we were at the hospital in Atlanta. He wanted to see me, but I told him I wasn't home. He told me to come home because it was important. I refused, so he sent me something."

I ran my hand between his shoulder blades, but it didn't seem to release any of his tension.

"What did he send you?"

"A video. A video of me...and him. Slade, I had no idea he'd done it. It's so embarrassing. He blindfolded me and told me to say certain things. Then he...we had sex. He filmed everything. And he's threatening to release the video on the internet unless we get back together."

So many feelings came over me, with the dominant one being anger at Richard the Fucking Tiny Dick for doing this to Aiden. For abusing his trust. For using it against him. For daring to threaten him.

Aiden had been carrying this anxiety on his own for ten days. No wonder he was at a breaking point.

"When is he expecting you?" I asked.

"I don't know. I was meant to have stopped for the night yesterday, so I guess...tonight? I wanted a few hours to get myself together before I got in touch with him."

"Do you think he'll release the video before he sees you?"

Aiden looked at me. His eyes full of fear, as if he hadn't considered that option, but then he said, "No, I don't think so. He wants money, so if he releases the video that's it, the video is out there."

"So he wants to keep the threat over your head, so you'll do anything he wants. Would he ever follow through on his threat?"

"Yes. If I push him far enough, he'll do it out of spite to ruin my reputation. This would ruin my parents' reputation too. We don't have the best relationship, but this could blacklist them from a lot of stuff they're involved with in New York. They mostly do charity work now, so this could have a bigger effect on the people they help."

I got up and walked around the room, trying to put my feelings aside so I could think straight. There was no way of telling how many copies of the video Dick had, and if there was more than one.

One thing was certain, I wasn't giving up Aiden for anything, so the moment Dick found out about us, he could well go off the rails and release the videos anyway.

"Okay, it's a wild shot, but I think there is someone who could help us," I said.

I grabbed my phone and sent Tom a message asking for his friend Connor's phone number. Connor's husband, James, had once been the bodyguard to the Prince of Lydovia, who happened to be married to Tom's best friend, Charlie. But my understanding was that before that he'd been some kind of computer whiz in the special forces.

I put the phone down while we waited for Tom's reply and then went over to Aiden, kneeling in front of him.

"Are you okay?"

He shrugged. "How did you get here? How did you know where I live?"

I chuckled. "You know airplanes travel faster than cars, right?"

"I thought you preferred riding."

"I do, but when there's something wrong with the love of my life, I'll fly, swim, run, walk, I'll do anything to get to you when you need me. Even when you don't tell me you need me."

"Wait...love of your..."

He widened his eyes and covered his mouth with his hand as he gasped.

"Oh my god, I totally threw myself at you last night, didn't I?"

"Uh huh." I pulled his hand down and replaced it with mine, tracing his soft lips. "And you told me you love me."

"I did...I mean...I do. I love you, Slade. So much."

I pressed my lips against his, feeling his warm breath on my skin. He put his hands on my face and pulled me closer, running his fingers down my beard. It was a tame kiss by all accounts, but it was by far the best kiss ever because it felt like coming home.

It was right, comforting, and it was Aiden.

"I love you too, Aiden. In case that wasn't clear by flying across the country to meet you or by telling you last night."

He laughed, and it was the best sound ever.

It was followed by my phone dinging with a message I hoped would help us get rid of Tiny Dick from Aiden's life once and for all.

I kept my eyes on Slade as he made the call to Connor.

My recollection of the night before was hazy at best, but I did remember declaring my love for him as soon as I saw him. I must have been in a state of delirium from overtiredness, but the words and the feelings were real. And he loved me too.

Now I could see how ridiculous it was that I ran away, but at the same time, acknowledging our feelings didn't make Richard's threat go away.

I had no solution for a way out other than give Richard what he wanted, as much as it would destroy me and Slade to do it. But maybe there was something.

Slade seemed to be speaking confidently to Connor, or maybe James. I couldn't get much from his side of the conversation.

"Babe, James wants to ask you some questions."

"Okay."

Slade passed me his phone.

"Hello?"

"Hi, Aiden, this is James. I'm really sorry this is happening to you. I'll do whatever I can to stop Pencil Dick from ruining your life. I just need some details, okay?"

"Sure, anything." I loved how everyone kept giving Richard those ridiculous nicknames. Under any other circumstances, I wouldn't encourage it, but it did make me feel like he had a little less power over me, just by the fact that no one respected him enough to ever use his name.

"I need to know a little about his shopping habits. Like what he buys online, what brands, etc."

"He likes to shop in person, but he will only buy socks from this online store that uses high quality cashmere. You can buy suits cheaper than a pair of those socks."

"That's great. Here's what we're going to do..."

I put James on speakerphone so Slade could hear it too.

The plan seemed fairly easy to execute, but the worst was that, in order for the plan to work, I'd need to have Richard over.

We ended the call after agreeing with James to lay low in the apartment and move my car so Richard wouldn't see it if he thought to come by. As far as he was concerned, I was still on the road, but there was no way to know if he'd checked up on the apartment or not. At least he didn't have a key, so he couldn't come in.

Thirty minutes later, Slade walked back into the apartment after moving the car. He was holding a shopping bag.

"What have you got there?" I asked.

He wiggled his eyebrows, taking a box of pancake mix, a bottle of chocolate sauce, and a squirt can of whipped cream out of the bag.

"No..."

I was still wearing the sweatpants I'd put on in panic earlier, but even my underwear was doing nothing to hide my hardness as Slade walked toward me, slowly removing his shirt.

"We have some time to kill, and you need breakfast," he said.

I walked slowly backward, biting my lip so I wouldn't moan at the sight of Slade removing his pants.

"And what are *you* going to have for breakfast?" I asked, even though I already knew the answer.

He crossed the space between us. "I'm going to have you."

A shiver of anticipation went down my spine. I ran toward the bedroom with Slade on my heels. He caught me by the waist and we both fell on the bed.

My clothes disappeared in a second and then there was only warm skin to warm skin.

He kissed a trail down my neck until he reached my chest. His beard tickled, which only served to heighten the sensation of Slade's teeth biting softly and then licking over my nipples.

I let out a moan and fisted the bedsheets.

"Hold that thought."

A minute later chocolate sauce dripped from the bottle onto my stomach, followed by a squirt of cream.

"You look delicious, baby. I might have to have a bite."

I couldn't even look at him. His eyes were on fire and his tongue worked me into a frenzy, and it wasn't anywhere near my cock.

"Please, Slade. If you love me just a tiny bit, you'll fuck me right now."

"Just a tiny bit? Babe, I love you more than love itself."

I sat up to kiss him and sighed when he followed me back to a lying position with him on top. His weight felt so good on me. His strong thighs against mine, the way his hair tickled me, and even though we were making a mess with the chocolate and cream, I didn't give a shit. I just wanted to feel him.

"Bedside table. Second drawer."

He looked at me. "What's in the top drawer?"

I bit my lips shut and smiled, shrugging innocently.

"Aiden...?"

He opened the top drawer and discovered my secret. Something I'd gotten a while ago but hadn't used.

"Why do you have a make-your-own-dildo kit in your drawer?"

"It was a joke gift from Wren...I never thought I'd get to use it, but now..."

I felt myself blush. Was I really going to confess it? He took a condom and lube from the second drawer and kneeled between my thighs.

"You have until I'm inside you to tell me what's in that sexy, dirty little head of yours."

I laid back down, moaning as Slade opened me with his fingers. How was I supposed to talk when he was doing *that* to me?

"Um...fuck, like that...Jesus, Slade...give me your big, fat cock," I demanded.

"Nuh huh, this isn't how it works."

I groaned. "Fine. First time we fucked, I thought that I'd do anything to have you in my mouth and my ass at the same time. There. Fuck me now."

His dick pressed against my hole, and I moved to bear down on it. I needed him so badly.

"So you're saying you want to make a mold of my cock," he said, pushing in a little farther. "So you can suck me," and a little more, "while I fuck you with the dildo of my cock?"

"Fuck, yeah," I moaned embarrassingly loud when he was all the way inside me. "God, I love your cock, Slade."

"It's a good thing I love your ass, baby. And you."

I couldn't tell how long we were like that for, him sliding in and out of me, slowly building up his speed as if we had all the time in the world.

Every time I was close to coming, he slowed down. I was going to punch him hard next time he referred to himself as old or lacking stamina. My legs were shaking and my body was sore, even though I was doing nothing else but taking him in, welcoming him, and letting him claim me.

I wondered if he'd be up to getting tested soon because I

wanted him with no barriers between us. The thought of fucking his ass without a condom was almost enough to bring on my orgasm.

"Fuck, baby, you feel so good."

I couldn't even speak. Nothing intelligible, at least.

"Hook your legs over my shoulders," he said between gritted teeth.

Good. I wasn't the only one struggling to keep going.

In this position we didn't have as much skin contact, but the angle was perfect for him to hit my spot. He wrapped his hand around my dick and stroked me in time with each one of his.

Ropes of cum covered my stomach as I gave in to my orgasm. Sparks danced in my eyes as blood rushed all over my body. Slade came a moment later, biting my calf as he emptied into the condom inside me.

He withdrew from me and then laid down next to me, pulling me in for a slow, languid kiss.

"I think we should take this into the shower," I said. Not that my legs had any will to move, but I was sticky with cum, chocolate, and cream. Debauched was an understatement for how I felt and looked.

Slade gave me a heated gaze full of promise. I just hoped James's plan worked and we could be happy together without any threat from Tiny Dick. And now even I was calling him by his nickname. Maybe having Slade here with me took some power away from Tiny Dick already.

"Hey," I said, scooting out of bed after Slade. "Is Liam still taking care of Harley? How often do you feed her? Last time she ate up the ham I brought her, as if it was going out of fashion."

"Huh?"

He looked puzzled.

"I'm confused that you seem confused."

"That's because I am. You know bikes run on gas, right?"

"Not the bike, dumbass. The cat."

"What cat?"

"Your cat."

He laughed.

"I don't have a cat."

"What?" I grabbed my phone from the bedside table and searched for the photo I'd taken of Harley asleep on top of a toolbox. "Yes, you do. This one."

Slade looked at the photo and laughed aloud.

"Babe, are you telling me that you've been feeding a stray cat all this time?"

"I didn't know she was a stray. She told me her name was Harley."

He laughed again, pulling me toward the bathroom.

"Sounds like you need feeding more urgently than I thought." He sprayed the warm water over me before using my shampoo to wash my hair. "Tell me, how did she tell you her name?"

I rolled my eyes. "I asked her if her name was Ginger, and she seemed offended by it and then she jumped on the bike, so I asked her if her name was Harley, and she meowed."

Okay, now that I said that aloud maybe it sounded a little weird.

He ran the water over my head to wash off the shampoo.

"I guess we're now the proud parents of a cat named Harley, aren't we?"

I shrugged. "I guess we are."

"Oh, Aiden, Aiden, what am I going to do with you?"

I ran my hands over the silver hairs on his chest. "I can give you an idea...or a hundred."

Slade's phone ringing in the bedroom put an end to our shower and brought back some of the anxiety that Slade had successfully banished.

Relief washed through me when James told us he'd successfully deleted all the videos from Richard's laptop and cloud. We just needed to execute part two of the plan, which unfortunately involved Aiden calling Richard to come over.

Aiden stilled when the intercom buzzed and looked at me like a deer in headlights.

"Hey, you're gonna be fine. You've got this."

"What if I can't get his phone?"

I'd pressed the buzzer to let Dick in the door downstairs, so we only had a minute. "Then we'll try again another time. It's unlikely he'll notice all the videos on his cloud are gone, so we have time."

I kissed him and went to hide in the spare room, leaving the door open a crack, so I could overhear them.

Moments later Aiden opened the door.

"Hey, beautiful. So glad to see you finally. You really could have made an effort to get home earlier. I missed you so much."

I clenched my fists until my knuckles were white and I felt

my nails bite into my palms. Even the guy's voice was annoying.

Calm down, Slade. We have a plan.

"Nice to see you too, Richard. Please come in."

"You don't look pleased to see me, honey."

I couldn't hear anything for a moment until Aiden replied, "I'm just tired from the trip, that's all."

"Anyway, I spoke to your mom yesterday and she's coming to visit soon. I think it's only wise that I move back in, don't you think?"

"Why?"

"You don't want her to think there's problems with our rekindled relationship, do you?"

I heard more movement, and from the small opening of the door, I saw Aiden move to the kitchen island. Perfect.

That's it, baby. You're doing well.

"Richard, we split up over a year ago. Do you think it's believable that we'd go straight back into a blissful relationship?"

Dick came into view. Aiden had shown me a photo of him, but in person he was even more sleazy than I'd imagined. The guy looked okay. Tall, with dark, styled hair, but when you're an ugly person on the inside, it doesn't matter how much you shine on the outside, you're still full of shit.

Aiden placed a glass of water on the island. He was keeping busy as I'd told him to because it would disguise any nerves.

Dick reached out for his hand. Aiden tried to pull back, but Dick held it.

"Baby, you have the perfect incentive, don't you? If you don't want your sick perversions to come out, you'll play nice with Mommy."

"Why are you doing this?" Aiden asked.

"Isn't it obvious?" He ran his finger up Aiden's arm.

He was lucky that they were on opposite sides of the

island, or I wouldn't be able to contain myself. Punching him until his nose needed corrective surgery was not part of the plan.

"Not to me, Richard."

"I loved you, Aiden. Even when you were a nobody. But you never listened to me. You could be even more than you are. Reach heights other authors in your genre could only dream to reach. It was as if you were allergic to making money."

Aiden shook his head.

"I made enough money, Richard."

"Only people with money say that, you privileged little brat."

Aiden flinched but held himself. We needed Richard to keep going.

"When you didn't want to follow my advice, I thought maybe we could get married. Have the lifestyle we dreamed of, the lifestyle we deserved. But you had to come out with that lie about your trust fund."

"I didn't—"

"Shut up," Dick said louder, placing his phone on the island. "I have it right here. I recorded a call with your mother in which she told me that wasn't true. In fact, you can access your trust fund any time you want. Isn't that right, Aiden dear?"

Aiden went around the island. "Is that what you want? Money?"

"No, Aiden. I want everything. You, your money, your lifestyle, your connections. I want the life I thought I was going to have when we first met, and I found out who you are."

Aiden's voice was low, but not low enough that I couldn't hear it. "Please forgive me. Please, Richard. You're right. I was selfish, and I was only thinking about myself. When we're in a relationship it's about us, both of us."

Aiden threw himself into Richard's arms and the fucker fell right into it.

"How about we make it right? Let's make it official. We'll ring my parents and set a date for the wedding."

Richard grinned. "Oh yeah?"

"Yeah...but first...how about we make it official in a different way?" Aiden's voice was sultry and low. "It's been a long time since we've been together. I miss you...all of you."

Aiden took Richard's hand and pulled him into the master bedroom. I hid behind the door of the guest room until it was safe to come out. As soon as I heard the hushed voices, I retrieved my phone from where it was recording the whole scene and stopped it. Then I grabbed Dick's phone, deleted all of his videos and photos and did a factory reset on it before I removed the sim card and snapped it in half.

Then I walked into the bedroom to claim my man. It was time to be a super, badass silver-fox biker as Aiden had called me.

As planned, Aiden had made his moves slowly, so he was still fully dressed. Richard had lost his shirt.

"You might want to leave now," I said.

"Who the fuck are you?" he asked. "Aiden, who the fuck is this? Call the police."

Aiden came over and put his arms around me. I felt all of his tension disappear like a cloud of smoke.

"This is my boyfriend. Please leave."

Dick's face went all red.

"Do you know what you're doing? I will come through on my threat. Just watch your precious reputation go down in tatters. Let's not mention Mommy and Daddy. All those poor loser kids they keep throwing money at? All gone at the touch of a button."

I held up his phone.

"You mean this button?"

I threw the phone at him and he scrambled to unlock it.

"Don't bother," I said with a chuckle. Aiden looked at me, and I nodded. It was done. All done, and he was free.

"What the fuck did you do, you asshole?"

Aiden moved so fast I couldn't hold him back. He grabbed Dick's shirt off the floor and threw it at him.

"You leave my house right now and never even think of me again. Since you won't have my number on your phone and your memory is shit, I know you won't call me."

Dick put his shirt on and walked toward the door, but he still wasn't ready to give in.

"Do you think I'm that stupid? I have more than one backup of these videos. This isn't over."

"That's where you're wrong, Dickhead," Aiden spat.

Go, baby. Was this the wrong time to get horny for my boyfriend?

"Buy any new socks today?" He asked.

Dick frowned.

"Thank you for giving us such easy access to everything on your laptop. We found some interesting things there. I'm not one for kink-shaming, but you have some fucked up stuff on there. Don't worry, we didn't delete it, we only made copies for ourselves."

Dick's face was a picture. I just put my hands in my pockets and enjoyed the show my man was delivering.

"Oh, you didn't think I could play the same game? I guess you underestimated the 'silly, overemotional romance author,' to quote your words. All the videos you made of me without my consent are gone. Do you know what will happen if you ever try to contact me?"

"You'll release the videos?"

"No, Richard. Unlike you, I wouldn't take something private and show it to the world. But I do have some interesting information about your work practices, your clients, and your finances, that I also copied from your laptop. If you ever come for me, that information will be handed to someone who will know exactly what to do with it. Somehow, I don't think seventy square feet is your idea of a nice retirement accommodation."

I walked around Aiden, stopping to kiss him on his head, and opened the door for Dick.

He walked away without looking back.

As soon as I closed the door, Aiden was on me. I took him by the backs of his legs until he wrapped them around my waist.

"You were fucking fantastic, baby. I'm so proud of you," I said.

"That was so nerve-racking, but it felt so good. Better would have been to punch him."

I laughed. "Not worth it. Besides, I can think of better things for you to do with your hands."

"Oh yeah?"

"Oh yeah.

AIDEN

"*B*abe?"

"One sec, just need to tuck this corner in," I said, pulling the white sheet tight under the mattress.

"Babe..."

His deep, husky voice was like a caress down my back and a stroke of my cock all in one. It was impossible to resist Slade. I didn't know why I'd even tried, because I'd been doomed to fail that particular objective from the get-go.

I turned around to see Slade wearing nothing but a towel around his waist, his chest hair still wet from his shower.

He ran his fingers through his hair and then down his face. His piercing blue eyes never left me as he stroked his beard before moving his hand farther down his stomach to where the towel was wrapped into a knot.

Fuck, he could put on a show.

"You know Tom and Wren will be here in a couple of hours."

"Uh huh."

He flipped the knot, but held it in a way that it all came undone while still covering his cock.

"Fuck, you're killing me, Slade. We have loads to do before they get here."

"Yeah, I know. You're too tense. I thought you could work some of that off...on me."

And then he dropped the towel onto the floor.

I groaned at the sight of his hard shaft, begging to be touched.

"Fine. But I'm not going to enjoy this."

He laughed. "Liar."

He was right. I was going to enjoy every single second of it.

I followed him out of the guest bedroom, where I'd been making the bed for our guests, and into the master bedroom.

"On your knees," I commanded.

He got up on the bed on all fours.

I was only wearing sweatpants, so I pulled them down and stepped out of them.

The bottle of lube was already on the bed.

In the last week we'd been tested and had received our results, but with putting my place up for sale and dealing with all the admin of moving my business to Chester Falls, we hadn't had energy for more than blowjobs or hand jobs in the shower.

Now it seemed my man needed more than a rushed orgasm. Well, we did have a couple of hours, and God had invented restaurants exactly for these times when we were too busy having sex to cook. True story.

I ran a finger up his thigh, teasing him. "You want me inside you, baby?"

"Fuck, yes."

His hole twitched in anticipation. I loved seeing him all open and ready for me. The trust he'd shown in me was humbling, and not only when it came to sex.

Now we knew everything about each other. There were no secrets, no skeletons, no lies. We knew each other, despite having only met weeks ago.

"Have you been getting yourself ready for me in the shower? Are you all nice and clean?"

"Yes."

Without any warning, I ran my tongue from his taint all the way up his crease.

"Oh, fuck," he moaned.

I used my hands to keep his ass cheeks apart so I could dive in, taste him, and show him how much I loved every single inch of him.

My cock was achingly hard, but I ignored it. I wanted him soft, relaxed, and ready for me.

"Aid. Please..."

His strained voice was music to my ears. I loved how he wasn't afraid to be vulnerable with me, wasn't afraid to love me and let me love him.

I grabbed the lube and ran a generous amount over my cock and onto his hole.

"Are you ready to take me?"

"Yes."

I pulled him back so his knees were on the edge of the bed and slowly eased myself inside him.

"God, you're tight."

"Just for you, baby."

I ran one hand up his back and kept the other on his hip to keep him in place.

"You love it when I take charge, don't you?"

"Yes."

"When I thrust inside you, filling you up and making you mine."

"Yes!"

"And you love it when I talk dirty, don't you?"

"Yes...fuck, yes!"

I held both his hands behind his back as I kept up a steady pace of hard thrusts. The only noises in the room were the slapping of skin against skin and his sharp intakes of breath.

There was no way to see his cock from where I was, but I imagined it was leaking like a tap. The way his moans were more and more broken told me how close he was.

I helped him straighten his back so he was against my chest, knees wide open, and head held back against my shoulder.

"Next time we'll have a mirror so I can watch you as you come apart. I want to see how much your cock leaks with every thrust—"

"Aiden..."

"Look at you, so beautiful, giving yourself to me. I will never take this for granted, Slade. I promise to always cherish every moment we have together."

"I love you so much, Aiden. So much."

He brought his arms around me from behind, so I kept one arm around his waist while I reached out for his cock. I gripped it tight as I drove into him harder until he shouted my name again as spurt after spurt of cum hit his chest and dripped down my hand.

My orgasm followed, hitting me with such force I had to lock my knees to stay upright.

We both collapsed on the bed, breathless and blissed out.

"We're gonna have to change the sheets again," I groaned. "This is all your fault."

He laughed and then stopped my protests with his mouth.

"How about a shower?"

"Yes, please," I agreed.

There was another small hurdle to face, which was to tell my parents about Richard's true intentions. Part of me didn't care if they believed me or not, but a bigger part of me wanted them to support me and be part of my life with Slade.

Freshly showered and with a coffee in my hand, I dialed my parents' number.

"Hello, Aiden, is that you?"

"Hi, Mom."

"What's going on, Aiden? Richard has been calling saying you're getting back together. That is excellent news. I'm so pleased for you—"

"Mom, I'm sorry to interrupt you, but Richard and I aren't back together, we never were and never will be."

"What do you mean?" She sighed. "Oh, Aiden, darling, when are you going to settle down?"

"Mom, I am settled. I am in love with a man that loves me in a way I never thought I deserved. He makes me feel worthy and capable."

"But what about Richard? We were so fond of him."

That was it. I took a deep breath and told her everything, leaving out only the blackmail video part. I'd use it if I needed to, but I was still embarrassed that I'd been put in that situation and wasn't ready to talk about it.

I offered to send her the footage from Slade's phone, but to my surprise, she told me it wasn't necessary.

"Sweetheart, we may not always approve of your choices, but you are our son. We just want to know that you're happy, and I'm sorry that we thought it would be with that man."

"Thank you, Mom. That...that really means a lot."

A lump formed in my throat. It had been a long time since I'd wanted to hug my mom this much.

"Hey, Mom, I don't suppose you and Dad would like to visit me and Slade at some point?"

"That would be wonderful, dear. Let me run it by your dad. You look after yourselves, okay?"

"Thanks, Mom."

Not long after, we were ready to receive our friends, and I was ready to say goodbye to San Diego.

"I hope you understand that us 'helping you move,'" Tom said in air quotes as soon as we opened my apartment door, "means me raiding *your* closet to make sure all the good stuff is transported safely into *my* closet."

Wren shook his head at his fiancé, even though nothing

but love shone through. Now I knew why everyone in our group of friends was so keen on pairing me and Slade up. Love really was the best thing ever.

"No." I pulled Harley into my arms. She came happily, nuzzling against my neck.

"But, babe, we can't really claim her as ours unless we know if she's chipped or registered somewhere."

"I don't care. No one's feeding her but us. I haven't seen any notices of people searching for a cat anywhere. She's ours."

Slade stared at Harley and me with raised eyebrows. Okay, so pouting wasn't working. Dammit.

He sat next to us and ran his hand over Harley's fur. She purred and went over to him. She always liked nuzzling under his beard.

Traitor.

I knew Slade was right, but I couldn't bear the thought of giving Harley to someone else.

We'd been back in Chester Falls for two weeks, and she'd become my writing companion. She'd sleep at my feet while I worked on my book, and then she'd follow me down to the garage and watch as Slade and I worked on the bike.

"If she was yours and you lost her, wouldn't you want to have her back?" he asked.

Damn him and his reasonable...reasoning.

"Okay, fine, but if she belongs to someone else, I'm going to buy her off them."

He chuckled and turned my face for a kiss.

Harley wasn't keen on PDAs unless they were directed at her, so she jumped off Slade's arms and went to hide in the bedroom.

With Slade's lap now vacant, I made my move.

"I believe this is how it all started," he said, running his hands over my jean-clad thighs.

I sighed. "I've thought back trying to find the defining moment that led me to being here with you, but I can't find it. It could have been the guy on the bike looking at the little girl that gave me the plot bunny for my book. It could have been the desperation to leave San Diego that brought me to Chester Falls. Maybe it was that split-second decision to help Ben out with the book fair. Or maybe it was the moment I was trapped in the intensity of your blue eyes."

He placed his hands on either side of my face and pulled me in for a gentle kiss. "You really are a writer."

I chuckled.

"Come on, let's take Harley to the V. E. T.," he said.

Tom had recommended Dr. Sawyer's practice, saying he'd been excellent with Coco, his and Wren's cat.

From the number of people in the waiting room with their pets, it looked like Dr. Sawyer was popular, or at least very good at his job.

Slade put his hand on my shaking leg.

"Sorry, I'm nervous for her. What if they hurt her?"

"They won't, baby."

I peered inside the travel box and Harley was happily asleep. To think our first encounter was her jumping on my back. She did have a naughty streak, but she seemed to pick her victims.

Liam often lost his lunch to mysterious events, but despite the warnings, he still made a habit of leaving his lunch on the bench while he answered the phone or saw a new customer in.

"Harley Warren-Lawton?" the girl in reception called.

"That's us."

We followed her to the consultation room.

"You gave the cat a hyphenated surname?" Slade asked.

"Of course. What else would she be called?"

"Hello, I'm Doctor Micah Sawyer, but you can call me Micah. Who do we have here?"

I looked at the doctor and then at Slade, who winked at me.

And now we knew why Tom had recommended this particular vet. Also why there was such a long line of mainly women with their pets outside.

"Hello, Micah. I'm Aiden, this is my boyfriend, Slade, and our daughter, Harley."

Slade coughed to disguise his laugh, but I didn't miss his look of pride when Harley didn't attack the vet. Maybe even she had a crush on him.

I mean tall, blond hair, green eyes. He had eye candy written all over him.

When Micah started his examination, my anxiety increased. Thank goodness Slade was there with me.

"Okay, so she's healthy and seems like a happy kitten. I'd say she's four, maybe five months old, and may have been the runt of the litter, which is why she's quite small. There's no chip on her either. I'm sad to say she may have been abandoned, but it seems like she's found a nice family to adopt."

Slade laughed. "You got that right."

Minutes later we left the practice as the official parents of Miss Harley Warren-Lawton.

I put my arm around Slade's waist while he had Harley in her carrier.

"I can't imagine life being more perfect than it is right now," I said.

"Not going to argue there, sweetheart."

We crossed the town square toward our street. I stopped and glanced around. It was another beautiful summer day. Soon it would be autumn and with it all the beautiful colors of the changing season.

"You know," I said, looking up at my gorgeous boyfriend, "after everything that happened with Richard, my parents, and when I couldn't write, I thought I just couldn't catch a break. But something—chance, fate, whatever—made me get into my car and drive. And look at me now. I caught myself a bunch of friends, a new home, and, more importantly, I caught myself a sexy silver-fox biker."

"Oh, Aiden...you caught my heart and soul when you saw me that first time. You caught me when I was falling, and I know you will for as long as we both shall live."

"You should put that in your vows," I said.

He widened his eyes and pulled me closer. "I hope that's you asking."

"I hope that's you saying yes."

~

Thank you so much for reading *How to Catch a Biker*, the fifth book in the Chester Falls series. Keep reading to get a special bonus scene.

Up next is *How to Catch a Vet*. Remember the sweet, popular Doctor Micah? He's a fairly new addition to town, and oh boy, will he be in trouble when he meets former soldier Santiago Torres.

Be sure to follow me on Bookbub to be notified of new releases, and look for me on Facebook for sneak peaks of upcoming stories.

Please take a moment to write a review of *How to Catch a Biker*. If you leave a review Slade will take you on a bike ride in the Connecticut countryside. (just keep your hands to yourself or Aiden might put you in a book and make bad things happen)

If you would like to be the first to know when my new releases are available, read exclusive FREE stories and know what I'm up to, please sign up for my newsletter, Ana's VIP Readers: *bit.ly/AnaAshley*.

For giveaways, sneak peaks, ARC opportunities and general caffeinated fun times, please join my facebook group! Café RoMMance - Ana's Reader Group.

BONUS SCENE

FINDING A NEW HOME

SLADE

My whole life, I thought riding was a solitary activity. I could ride with hundreds of other bikers, but every time I was on a bike, I was in my own world, my bubble.

Being aware of the people around me, communicating with them, or following the crowd didn't diminish the fact that it was just me on my bike.

That was until Aiden came along.

Riding with Aiden had become such an experience that I didn't think I'd ever go back to riding a bike alone. I didn't even have the desire to.

And when it came to the actual riding, like in bed, we were happy to switch.

Had I been abducted by mind-altering aliens that brainwashed me into giving up control? Maybe. I liked to think I'd simply found someone I could trust with my life and heart.

That thought made me sad for the years I'd been with Mike.

I'd loved him then, and I still loved him. Would our lives

have turned out differently if I'd met him under different circumstances? At a different time in my life?

Maybe...maybe not.

As much as I regretted not being the man Mike had needed me to be, I couldn't regret any of my past decisions that eventually led me to this moment.

Aiden held on to me as I took us down the country roads to our spot. The spot I'd used to clear my mind in the past, but that had forever changed when we had our first kiss there.

Summer was coming to an end, but the cooler temperatures didn't change our plans.

Now that the Harley was fully restored, we were going on a riding vacation in a week.

The journey was unknown. The goal was to enjoy ourselves and see some cool sights along the way. The destination? Well, that was up to Aiden if I ever got the guts to ask him the question I'd been meaning to for a while.

"You okay, baby?" I said into the Bluetooth intercom device.

"Yeah."

He was squirming a little on his seat, so I wondered if I'd been rougher with him last night than I'd thought.

Not that he complained since he'd more or less begged me for a second go as soon as he came down from his first orgasm.

The downside of my age was that recovery took a lot longer. The benefit was that I could get Aiden off a second time and sometimes even draw a third orgasm from him.

Today's ride was just a test to see how the Harley performed. We'd taken it around town but hadn't had the chance for a longer ride, and since we'd soon be spending many hours on it, I wanted to ensure it was up for the challenge.

As usual, no one was on the dirt road, but after some research, I now knew why that was the case. Nerves settled in my stomach as we approached our parking spot.

I was thinking about our future together, and for the first time in my life, my future included more than a good bike and an open road.

A side effect of having Aiden holding on to me while we were on the bike was that I couldn't wait to touch him back. So as soon as we were both off the bike and our helmets were off, I put my arms around him and claimed his mouth.

I was happily lost in him when I felt something move in his backpack.

One of Aiden's cutest habits was to carry a notebook everywhere so he could jot notes when something inspired him. I'd even gotten him a small backpack to hold his things when we traveled. A backpack that now seemed to be alive.

"Aiden?"

"Hmm?"

He didn't meet my eyes.

"Is there something you want to tell me?"

He shook his head.

"Are you sure?"

He raised his eyes slowly. The blush on his cheeks was adorable, and I was so tempted to go back to kissing him, but...a familiar sound came from his backpack.

I raised my eyebrows.

"I can explain," he said.

"This will be interesting." I chuckled.

He took off his backpack and opened it to reveal Harley curled up inside. She scrambled out of the bag and jumped onto my shoulder when she saw me.

"She wanted to come along," Aiden said.

"Oh, really? And you know this because...?"

"She told me."

"Right..."

Harley meowed again. I crossed my arms so she could get into her favorite position between my neck and my beard. If she'd endured a bike ride in a dark bag, this was the least I could do for her.

"It's true. I was getting my notebook, and she jumped in the bag and wouldn't get out. I had no choice." He shrugged.

I laughed loudly and put one arm around him, pulling him close so I could kiss his head.

"Nothing to do with you wanting to bring her along on our trip?"

He huffed, knowing he'd been caught.

When we'd talked about the trip, understandably, Aiden hadn't wanted to leave Harley behind. She was an important part of our family.

Hell, she ran our family.

The problem was keeping her safe while we traveled. A short ride in a backpack wouldn't do her harm, but a longer trip wouldn't be as comfortable, so we'd agreed to leave her with Tom, Wren, and their cat, Coco.

Coco and Harley often had playdates and got along very well, so we knew she'd be safe and happy.

I shook my head. "You're lucky I love you so much. Both of you."

"Does that mean she can come with us on our trip?"

Could I ever deny this man anything?

"I guess she is."

He raised his hand, and Harley bumped it with her paw.

Great, this is how it all starts.

And I'd be damned if it didn't make my heart even fuller than it was. If I wasn't careful, I'd be a walking, talking pile of lovey-dovey mush.

If Ted could see me now.

I looked up at the blue sky. If Ted was watching, I hoped he knew how loved he was and how much he was missed.

"Come on, guys, let's go," I said, pulling Aiden with me.

"Wait, where are we going? Isn't the overlook to Reed's

farm that way?" Aiden asked when he figured out we were heading in the opposite direction.

"It is, but there's something I want to show you first."

It was a good fifteen-minute walk, and eventually, Harley was tired of being carried and decided to explore the area. She was always near us, so I wasn't worried about her getting lost.

She was a feisty and fearless kitten, but she was loyal and very protective of us.

The house looked much nicer in real life than in the photos I'd seen online.

A farmhouse with a wraparound porch, a small barn that could be converted into a garage, plenty of land, and a surprise addition that had made me go from looking at the listing to contacting the seller.

"What's this?" Aiden asked. "Can we be here?"

"We can. This house and the surrounding property, including our spot overlooking Reed's farm, are up for sale. The owner is moving to the city to live with his grandson, and he's looking to sell to someone who will make this a home and look after it, make memories, and maybe one day pass it down to a new generation."

Aiden looked at me. His eyes were wide and welling up.

"Are you saying...are you...do you want to live here?" he asked.

"Only if you do too. Our spot would be ours forever. There's plenty of land for Harley to explore, and who knows, maybe one day, we can be adopted by another kitten or a dog. Maybe even children?"

"Oh, Slade."

Aiden slammed into me, holding me tight.

I held him right back.

When he pulled away, his eyes were red.

"What's the matter, baby?"

"Do you really want kids?"

Ah, so that's what it was. I cleared his tears and kissed him.

"I didn't think I did, but I also never thought I'd be so happy with the life we have. When I see you with Harley, sometimes I wonder what it would be like if we had a kid of our own...I just..."

He placed his hands on my face, so I leaned down for a kiss.

"Slade, I think I'd like to adopt an older child. Someone who, for whatever reason, doesn't have a family of their own. We can be their family."

"Damn you, Aiden, you're gonna make me cry."

"That's okay. You're old, so I know emotions can get the best of you."

I slapped his ass, but he got away from me. I chased him until he was back in my arms again.

"So, what do you say?"

"Yes."

"To what?"

He gave me his smile that lit up my life every time I saw it.

"To the house, to adopting a kid. Hell, I'll even marry you if you ask."

"Will you?"

It was scary how my life had become so perfect that even this moment couldn't have been better planned.

"Will I what?" Aiden asked, his hands shaking against my chest.

"Will you marry me?"

He nodded fiercely. "Yes, definitely. Yes...did I say yes yet? Because it's a yes."

I put my hand inside my leather jacket and felt for the hidden pocket keeping the rings safe since I got them a month ago.

"Well, in that case, you better have this," I said, placing one of the rings on his finger.

"Oh my god. Slade, you were planning this?"

"I've had the rings for a while. I was waiting for the right moment, and hearing you talk about giving a kid like me a chance to have a family...the same chance I once had... I fall in love with you every single day as soon as I open my eyes and stare into your sleepy, beautiful face. But when you say things like what you just did, you make me fall even deeper. There will never be a way back for me, Aiden."

"Good. I'm not letting you go anywhere."

Harley came back from her explorations and jumped on us.

Aiden rubbed her ginger fur, and she purred.

"Come on, let's go to our spot because I'm going to give Daddy an alfresco blowjob," he said.

Harley jumped back to the ground, clearly not impressed.

"Hold that thought. I want to show you something first."

I took his hand and led him around the house. The owner had told me he was with his grandson this weekend, but we were free to walk around and explore. We could always come back another day to see the inside of the house.

There was a large grassy area behind the house, and at the end was a path cut between the trees. We followed it, and sure enough, there it was.

"Oh my god, Slade. This is...I don't even know how to describe it."

The stream wasn't deep or wide, but it flowed well. The owner told me the water never dried up, but it did get a little deeper in the winter with rain and snow. It was perfectly safe, and there was no risk of flooding the house.

"Do you like it?" I asked.

"Yes, this is so beautiful, so peaceful."

"I was thinking we could build a small cabin here. Just one room with running water and power so you could set up your office here."

Aiden stood in front of me. The way he was biting his lip told me his thoughts weren't entirely pure.

"So...if my office was here," he said, running his hands

down my chest and around my back, settling over my ass. "It would be a little lonely...you know...just me and this beautiful view."

I smiled.

"I could visit you."

"You mean like conjugal visits?"

"This isn't a prison, baby."

He closed his hands over my ass, pulling us even closer. I felt his erection against mine.

"But what if I accidentally, while researching a book, of course..."

"Of course..."

"What if I accidentally handcuffed myself to my strong wooden desk, and I couldn't reach the keys?" He kissed my neck, licking a path to my earlobe. "Would you come rescue me?"

I swallowed as his warm breath tickled my skin.

"You know I'm good with tools."

He snorted. "What would you do to me with your tools?"

"I think helping you out of the handcuffs wouldn't be the first thing I'd do," I said.

He cupped my erection before searching for the buttons on my jeans.

"I like that. I'd be at your mercy. You could do whatever you wanted to me."

"Tell me. Will your office come with supplies?" I asked.

He popped a button open.

"You mean stationery?"

"No, baby. Lube."

He popped two more buttons and returned to kissing my neck, biting my Adam's apple and then sucking a patch of skin.

I groaned.

"You can bet all the tools in your garage that lube will be

the first item inside the cabin as soon as there are four walls and a roof."

He got on his knees and took my cock out. I felt the cool air for less than a second before the wet heat of Aiden's mouth covered my cock.

I knew we were alone, but seeing Aiden on his knees like that, so lost in our pleasure that he didn't care if anyone saw us, threatened to make me come undone.

"Fuck, baby. You look so beautiful like that."

He moaned around my cock, sucking the crown before taking as much of it as he could.

I ran my hands through his hair and pushed it away from his eyes. I wanted to look at him, see the man I'd fallen in love with. The man I was going to marry.

He licked the length of my cock and then sucked my balls. My eyes rolled back from the pain-pleasure of his mouth sucking and tugging.

"Ngh...fuck..."

Knowing we were the only people for miles didn't mean I felt comfortable letting go and shouting my pleasure. Maybe one day, when this place was truly ours, we could lie here by the stream on a blanket, making love to each other and then sleeping under the stars.

Aiden opened the zip of his jeans and stroked his own hard cock. I knew if he was doing that, he must be close.

"I'm right there with you, baby. Just let me know where to come," I said.

"My mouth. I want to swallow every last drop."

I was blind to the world around us as I gazed into his eyes, seeing as they went darker the closer he got to his orgasm.

He didn't stop sucking my crown or stroking me with his free hand until he froze for a moment, and I knew he was coming, even though I couldn't see it.

His eyes rolled, and there was so much bliss on his face.

"Baby..." That was the only warning I gave before my orgasm crashed over me.

As promised, he drank every single drop.

I went down to the grass, counting my blessings that it was dry, and pulled Aiden into my arms.

"This was not part of today's plan, but fuck, baby. You and that mouth of yours," I said, still trying to get my heartbeat back to a more regular pattern.

He chuckled against me. "I could fall asleep right now."

"Probably not a wise thing. And especially not while we both have our dicks out."

"Then let's get up because I'm not making any promises."

We walked back toward the house, admiring the yard. It didn't have any particular features, which made sense, considering the current owner probably wasn't healthy enough to tend to flower beds.

I noticed a few things that would need attention, but this was a place we could make a home in.

"What if he doesn't want to sell us the house?" Aiden asked.

"I've already spoken to the owner and his grandson. I made a hypothetical offer to gauge their interest, and they said if we made that offer formally, they'd accept it."

"Let's do it."

What I liked most about the house and the price the sellers were willing to accept was that it was something both Aiden and I could afford without touching his family's money.

We didn't talk about it much, mostly because it always ended in an argument, and I had strong beliefs about stuff we should buy for ourselves and how his money should be used.

Aiden's biker book had just been released, and his readers had gone crazy for it. It seemed that his hiatus caused an issue of supply and demand.

His PA insisted he continue with a series of biker-themed

books, which was fine by me. I was more than happy to help him with his research.

Aiden was enjoying getting his writing mojo back. Whenever he decided to take a break to focus on other things, he already had charity projects lined up. His money would go to good causes and people that really needed it.

"How about the apartment?"

"What?"

"What are you going to do with the apartment?"

I grabbed his hand and laced our fingers together. "I was thinking we could keep it as a crash pad. Stay there whenever we want to go out in town so we don't have to ride back, especially if we drink."

"Hmm...or maybe...sometimes I might get stuck and need help getting unstuck up there. I hear mechanics are good with their tools."

I laughed. "Our hands too." I wiggled my brows.

Harley caught up with us just as we got back to the bike.

Like the first time we rode together, I picked up Aiden's helmet and put it over his head, tightening it for him.

With Harley back in the backpack, we were ready to ride back to Chester Falls and into our future together.

PREVIEW OF HOW TO CATCH
A VET

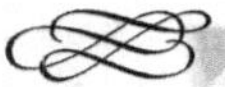

MICAH

"Hey, Dad. Hey, Mom," I said into the screen.

"Happy anniversary, sweetie," they both sang.

God, I missed my parents. Only they would celebrate the one-year anniversary of the opening of my vet practice. Because it's a milestone, and they love a celebration.

"Thanks. How are you doing? I see the weather is great out there, as always."

I saw the pool and the clear blue sky behind them, and I was only ten percent jealous because summer had arrived in Chester Falls, but sadly, I had no pool.

"We're wonderful, sweetie. You could have this too. We told you to sell the house and open up here. You'd be closer to us."

"I know, Mom, but Florida is *your* dream, and I've always loved it here. I'm happy being back home. Reopening Grandpa's practice is a dream come true. I have so many plans for this place."

They looked at each other, and I knew they would love to have me there but were also happy with my decision.

"He'd be very proud of you, Micah," my dad said.

"Thanks, Dad. I think so too."

"Doctor Sawyer, your next patient is here," my assistant called from the door.

"Thanks, April. Send them in, please," I said.

I closed down the tab on my computer where, before my parents called, I'd been drafting the third email to the construction company that I'd hired to build my animal sanctuary.

"Mom, Dad, I have to go. I'll speak to you soon, okay? Love you."

There was a knock on the door, followed by one of my favorite four-legged patients and her dad.

"Micah, I was telling April how I think you need a little bit of color in your reception area. Maybe some pictures of pets on the walls and sparkle. You definitely need some sparkle. I read about this paint you can use that has glitter in it—it's very safe and nontoxic—and it would be perfect for one of the walls. The animals would love it. I bet they'd be less scared of coming to the doctor if they were distracted by something pretty. I mean, April is lovely, but you know, she doesn't quite...sparkle."

I bit the inside of my cheek to stop myself from laughing aloud.

"Hi, Tom, how are you doing?" I asked, taking the kitten carrier from him and placing it on the examination table.

He let out a big sigh. "Oh, you know. I always get a little nervous when I bring her in."

"There's no need. You take really good care of her. I'm sure there's nothing to worry about. Unless you've noticed any change in her behavior pattern, sleep, or eating?"

It was normal for the owners to be more nervous around vets than their pets, so I liked to reassure them. But there was always the possibility that pets could develop a condition or illness that could go undetected until they came for the annual check.

"No, she's the same old queen of the castle and owner of my heart," he said, looking at Coco adoringly.

"And what does Wren think about that?" I said, raising a brow.

"Oh, he knows," Tom said, waving it off. "There's plenty of love in my rainbow heart for my little girl and my big man."

I laughed. Tom's fiancé, Wren, went to my high school, and even though we were in different years, I remembered the popular football player who I'd admired from afar. Tall, with a broad back and muscles for days, physically, he was totally my type. He'd been one of the reasons I'd realized I was into guys rather than girls, even though he wasn't out then.

I opened the door to the carrier, and Coco came out, going straight to her dad for a nice rub before coming to me.

"Good morning, Princess. How have you been since the last time I saw you?" I cooed, and she gave me a good sniff before deciding I was worthy enough to rub her white belly. "Good girl."

While I petted her, I felt for her organs in order to assess whether they appeared to be normal and for evidence of discomfort. I also checked the general condition of her hair-coat, which was as I expected, and the same for her skin.

"No signs of excessive oiliness or dryness, no dandruff..." I muttered to myself aloud, more for Tom's benefit than my own.

I grabbed a wriggly toy to play with to check her general level of alertness and interest in her surroundings and her muscle condition. Everything seemed to be good.

"Look, Coco, what's that on there?" I said, adding a spoonful of cat food to the base of the weighing scales.

Her healthy sense of smell meant she more or less leaped onto the scales.

"That would be the only way you'd get me on a set of scales too," Tom said, chuckling.

Not that he needed to worry about that, I thought. He looked perfectly proportionate, considering his petite frame.

Now I, on the other hand, definitely needed to lose some weight. Despite my height, I'd never been a slim guy, and the stress of moving back to Chester Falls and setting up my practice had me slacking in my meal planning. And that was when I actually had a proper meal. Apparently, eating ice cream while watching old reruns of *The Golden Girls* does not constitute a balanced diet.

"Her weight is ideal for her age," I said. "She's perfectly healthy, Tom."

He let out a visible sigh of relief.

"See, baby? I told you there was no reason to worry," he cooed at Coco, who was back in his arms, resting her head on his shoulder and purring away happily.

"Let's just give her the annual shots, and you'll be good to go."

Despite using my best tricks, Coco was not best pleased with me after getting her shots. Even another spoonful of food didn't convince her I wasn't the evilest human on the planet.

Fortunately for me, she was an extremely social kitten, and I'd bet my degree that she'd run to me for a belly rub the next time I walked past Tom's store, Fabulize.

"Thank you so much, Micah," Tom said when Coco was settled back in her carrier.

"It's my pleasure. See you around."

My schedule looked clear for at least thirty minutes, so I walked to the reception area to see if April wanted me to fix her a coffee while I grabbed a quick lunch upstairs.

I nearly bumped into Tom, who was staring at the walls with a curious look.

"Tom, is everything okay? Did you forget something?"

"Oh, no, I was just memorizing your layout so I can draw you a nice plan."

I smiled. "I don't think I can afford to have any work done out here, Tom. As much as I appreciate—"

A gasp from April made us both turn. She had a paper in her hand and had gone as white as a ghost.

"April, are you okay?"

She looked at me slowly and handed me the paper.

"I was opening today's mail..."

My eyes landed on the words *bankruptcy matter,* and my stomach dropped, making me feel sick. I tried to calm down and read the rest of the letter to make sure I didn't misunderstand the situation.

Please be advised that this firm has been retained to represent the above-referenced debtors for the purposes of bankruptcy filing under Chapter 7 of the United States Bankruptcy Code.

It was all gone. The money my grandad had left me. It was all gone. The contracting company had filed for bankruptcy, and it was unlikely I'd ever see any of that money again.

"Micah, what's going on?" Tom asked, his voice laced with worry.

"I feel so stupid," I said, holding on to the letter as if I could will the words to disappear.

"What do you mean?"

"The contractors said I had to pay for the work up front because they're a small company and couldn't afford to buy the materials before getting paid. I should have known better."

The door to the practice opened, so I turned to go back into the consultation room. I couldn't have my patients see me like this. I needed to pull myself together and think about this later.

A hand on my arm stopped me.

"Hey, it's only Wren. You're among friends," Tom said gently.

I nodded and went over to the chairs in the waiting area and sat down.

"April, can you call up the nearest animal sanctuaries and

check what their situation is? We may need to call on them for help. And we'll need to find forever homes for the ones we have in the backyard because we don't have anywhere suitable enough to keep them over the winter months."

"Of course, doctor. I'll get right on it."

Tom sat next to me. "Is there anything we can do to help?"

"No, unless you know of people looking to offer a bunch of perfectly imperfect pets a forever home."

He gave me a wide smile. "Leave it with Uncle Tom."

"Oh, boy," Wren said. "Here we go again."

Tom gave Wren a murderous look, and I managed a laugh when Wren looked terrified, but soon enough, Tom was walking into his arms and asking for lunch.

"Honestly," Wren said to me, "we'll speak to everyone we can. I see the parents after football practice most days, so I can mention you have some pets up for adoption."

"It's not that easy, Wren. Some of the animals have special needs. That's why they're here and not in someone's home. They were either found abandoned on the side of the road or left here because they have complex medical needs."

"Like I said. We'll do what we can."

I nodded and smiled.

Chester Falls was one of those rare places where people knew and helped each other. Or at least that's how it had been when I was growing up.

I could only hope the same community spirit still prevailed in Chester Falls, because now I had no idea how I could build a weatherproof shelter to keep the animals through winter.

CONNECT WITH ANA

Connect with Ana on social media:

Hang out in my FB Group:
facebook.com/groups/CafeRoMMance
Follow me on instagram: *instagram.com/anawritesmm/*
Follow me on Bookbub: *bookbub.com/authors/ana-ashley*
Sign up to my newsletter: *bit.ly/AnaAshley*

For an overview of all of Ana's books and audiobooks, visit her website: *anawritesmm.com/books*

BOOKS BY ANA ASHLEY

Single Dads of Stillwater
A spin off series from Chester Falls that can be read on its own. Each book features one or more single dads in this community of friends, family and found family. In this contemporary MM romance series you'll find heat, emotion and a guaranteed happy ever after.
Newcomer
Antagonist
Breakthrough
Heartstring
Datebook (Coming early 2024)

Finding You Series
A standalone series set across the Atlantic between New York and Portugal. Find your way home with this contemporary MM romance series with friends to lovers, star-crossed lovers and age gap with plenty of heat, feels and always a happy ever after.
Home Again
Together Again
Love Again
And for a special short story, Complete Again, plus bonus scenes, grab the Finding You boxset now.

Room for 3 series
This is a high heat MMM contemporary romance series set in an island resort.
The Resort
The Vacation (Free short story)

Chester Falls Series
From a Prince to a Happy Ever After for all, enjoy this small town MM romance series that's as sweet as they come, with plenty of heat, humor and everything in between.
How to Catch a Bookworm (Prequel short)
How to Catch a Prince
How to Catch a Rival
How to Catch a Bodyguard
How to Catch a Bachelor

How to Catch the Boss (a Christmas novella)
How to Catch a Biker
How to Catch a Vet
How to Catch a Happy Ever After
You can now have all the books in the series and the prequel all in two boxsets.
Chester Falls Collection Volume I
Chester Falls Collection Volume II

Standalone books
Christmas Bubble: a low angst, standalone, Christmas novel featuring a petite but larger-than-life cheerleader, an older demisexual football coach and a winter cabin by the lake with only one bed. With cameos from Chester Falls and Stillwater.
Midnight Ash: a sweet Cinderella fairytale retelling with a sexy kinky twist on the side, and a cast who don't quite behave as you'd expect.
Stronghold: a sweet and sexy romance in Sarina Bowen's World of True North, Vino & Veritas series. This is a standalone story between two childhood friends who reunite after as decade apart, with some creative use of maple syrup.

FREE READS
My Fake Billionaire
The Vacation

ABOUT ANA

Ana Ashley was born in Portugal but has lived in the United Kingdom for so long, even her friends sometimes doubt if she really is Portuguese.

After getting hooked on reading gay romance, Ana decided to follow her lifelong dream of becoming an author.

These days you can find her in front of her laptop bringing her stories to life, or in the kitchen perfecting her recipe for the famous Portuguese custard tarts.

Ana Ashley writes sweet and steamy gay romance set in America, often in small towns where everyone knows everyone.

~

You can follow Ana on the usual social media hangouts.

For access to exclusive teasers, content, and general book and food related goodness you can now join Ana in her Facebook Group, Café RoMMance - Ana's Reader Group

Ana's VIP Readers - bit.ly/AnaAshley

Facebook Page - @anawritesmm

Email - ana@anaashley.com

Instagram - @anawritesmm

Bookbub - bookbub.com/authors/ana-ashley

Goodreads - goodreads.com/ana-ashley

www.ingramcontent.com/pod-product-compliance
Lightning Source LLC
Chambersburg PA
CBHW020748190726
48285CB00006B/1937